A Mother's Boy

A Mother's Boy

Colin Walker

CONNOLLY & WILSON
Publishers

First published in the United Kingdom
in 2006 by Connolly & Wilson.

The characters and situations in this book
are wholly fictitious, any resemblances to actual
people or events being unintentional.
Where names replicate those of actual people,
locations or organisations, the author apologises
for any displeasure occasioned by the coincidence.

The moral right of the author has been asserted.

ISBN 10 0-9535655-3-X
ISBN 13 978-0-9535655-3-5

Jacket design by J.I. Stanway.
Produced by
Action Publishing Technology Ltd,
Gloucester GL1 5SR
Printed and bound in Great Britain

For Malcolm Sheppard

And yet how few there are from whom one would not
get some queer reaction if one knew the right
word, the right gesture!

André Gide,
The Vatican Cellars

Each had his past shut in him like the leaves of
a book known to him by heart; and his friends
could only read the title.

Virginia Woolf

Chapter One

Suddenly she was beside him, astride a skittish palomino whose gold and silver beauty increased Bruce's dissatisfaction with the elderly black mare he had been assigned. He had noticed neither palomino nor rider when, in company with a dozen or more Sunday regulars, he was mounting and waiting in the stable yard. Now, in warm autumn sunshine, the riders were out on the Cheshire Plain, following a leader in rising trot and chatting between themselves.

She said: 'That's Daisy you're riding, isn't it? Not the freshest of daisies at End Point Riding Centre, but probably the safest. How d'you find her?'

'Slow, jaded and thoroughly fed up with beginners like me. I'm forty,' Bruce admitted. 'I've concluded that those riders who look as if they're part of the horse are the ones who learnt to ride when they were young and unafraid.'

'Like my son. Right now, while his father and I are out hacking, he's having his lesson in the indoor school. Monty's eleven. I won't let him join us till I'm satisfied with his control.'

'I should do more school work myself, but I'm only a fun rider. I'll never make Badminton.'

'I haven't seen you at End Point before.'

'I just have an hour in the school most Friday nights and then this Sunday hack.'

'Righty. Clyde and I normally go out with the three o'clock, but this week we had to change our arrangements and join this earlier one. I'm Estelle Beaumont.'

'Cameron. Bruce Cameron. I've been admiring your horse.'

'You should be admiring me. His name's Cromwell. A half-thoroughbred. I bought him at the right price from a man who was going to prison.'

'I guessed it wasn't a school horse. D'you groom him yourself? Some owners do, I'm told.'

Estelle laughed. Cameron liked her. She was a pretty woman. Her features were small and neat, her brown hair worn short and softly waved, her nose straight and slender. It was a face that radiated serenity and confidence, an honest face that hid nothing except a fierce temper.

'Cromwell's at full livery,' she explained, 'along with Clyde's gelding, perversely named Countess, which suggests a sex-change somewhere down the line. We just ride them. End Point staff do the work, including exercising them when we're not riding ourselves.'

'Where's your husband now?'

'Clyde's in back somewhere. You're a novice, you say. What made you take up riding, Bruce?'

Cameron hesitated, a little surprised at being called Bruce. The year was 1984 and the practice of immediate first-naming had yet to establish itself in Britain.

He said: 'I needed something new – something to add to jogging, squash and shooting. I considered pimping, stalking, demanding money with menaces, and finally chose riding.'

In truth, there had never been a contest. Cameron had started riding because he wanted to be ordered about in the school by a girl with a whip in her hand.

2

'I can see you're bursting with fitness,' Estelle said, smiling her approval. 'Very trim. Very muscular. Shall I tell you who you remind me of, Bruce?'

'Dame Nellie Melba.'

'Tyrone Power.'

'A man once came up to me on Paddington Station. *"General Smuts?"* he began. *"No"*, I said. *"You're not half like him"*, the man said, peering at me. *"That fits"*, I answered. *"He's been dead and buried for fifty years"*.'

'Tyrone Power had your black hair, dark eyes and square face. Considered among the most handsome of Hollywood stars. What we call a studmuffin, which means athletic and sexually dangerous. How come you're not married, my friend?'

'Who said I'm not?'

'All your pursuits are solitary. A widower perhaps.'

'Bachelor. I'm single because I've never met anyone I wanted to marry or who wanted to marry me.'

'I don't believe that. It's my guess a lot of women have been in love with you.'

'People marry for companionship or to have children. I want neither. I have my job and what you call my pursuits and that's all I want.'

Estelle, smiling indulgently this time, told Bruce he was a selfish old bachelor. He replied: 'What could be more selfish than parenthood? Unless they were mad, your parents didn't say to each other "The world is so wonderful that we'd be criminals not to bring a child into it". Of course they didn't. They just wanted a child.'

'Or maybe they didn't, but got one just the same.'

'Before parents accuse me of being selfish, they should compare my taxes with theirs and thank me for supporting their offspring.'

'Will you always be a bachelor boy, Bruce? Will you go to your grave wondering, even perhaps sorrowing?'

'I liked the word bachelor even as a boy. There's a

3

song, isn't there, called *A Bachelor Gay*? I think it's from *The Maid of the Mountains*. I remember my sister, Joan, calling me in from the garden when it came on the radio. It was my favourite. The use of the word gay to describe male homosexuals probably derives from it, because to the simple mind all bachelors are homo.'

'Are you, Bruce?'

'No.'

'Sure?'

'If I were homosexual, I'd desire other men. Right?'

'Righty.'

'Well, I don't, so I'm not. I'm a loner, okay, but neither homo nor this-way-that-way.'

'We all contain sexual pressure that must be released,' said Estelle, 'either with a partner of the same sex or of the opposite sex or with children or animals.'

'Some people are content to take themselves in hand.'

'Is that you, Bruce? Is solitary pleasure your safety valve?'

'Sometimes. Mostly, I meet girls at dances and take them back to my bungalow in Hurworth. I'm not a drinker or a socialiser. If I can get my leg over once in a while, that's all I want.'

'What d'you call dancing? Standing facing your partner and snapping your fingers at her?'

'Ballroom. Latin. I like discipline, precision, exercise.'

'You should have been a soldier boy.'

'I'd like to have been a bodyguard.'

At a call from the leader, the riders sank from rising to sitting trot and then to walk. Cameron was relieved. He was out of breath. Beginner that he was, he put more effort into riding than his horse did, whereas Estelle Beaumont, relaxed and smiling, left Cromwell to get on with it.

4

He turned and looked to the rear and decided that Clyde Beaumont was the man trailing behind the others, his obvious discomfort suggesting that he would rather be anywhere than in the hack. He was scrubbing the saddle, as the End Point teaching staff would have said, meaning his seat was yet sloppier than Bruce's, rendering his control, even in walk, almost non-existent.

Estelle said: 'You're ripe for marriage, you know. All you're waiting for is the woman who knows the right words.'

It was a bizarre comment, a shot in the dark, and it brought Cameron up short. He wanted to hear more. 'What are they?' he asked, warily, as if he didn't know.

'They differ from person to person. Don't be discouraged.'

'Who said I am?'

'Always think in terms of success, Bruce.'

'Listen to this. I recently cancelled one of my charge cards. The company bombarded me with reasons why I should continue with it. I hit on a way of shaking them off. I wrote to tell them I was out of work and saw little chance of getting another job. Not another word. "Nothing succeeds like failure", I said to myself. But I accept what you say. I'm a salesman and a salesman has to think in terms of success.'

'Call me Estelle instead of just nothing all the time.'

'Estelle.'

'I like my name. It looks French, whereas I'm told it's a Charles Dickens invention, slightly modified. It's nice and feminine, isn't it? Do you like your name?'

'Can't say I ever think about it. I don't like unisex names, like Evelyn or Hilary. I grew up in a world where girls were girls and boys were boys and both sides appreciated the difference. Today, unfortunately, girls are copying boys to the point where you can hardly tell them apart.'

5

'What makes a salesman, Bruce? Come on! What are the ingredients?'

'The textbooks say he must be a blend of optimist, psychologist and actor. He must never be insincere or dismissive of rivals and their products. Quite apart from the fact that it's bad manners to run down a competitor, he should remember that he may be working for them one day and customers have long memories.'

'Keep your words soft and sweet,' Estelle said, 'because you never know when you may have to eat them. Are you a good salesman, Bruce?'

'Adequate. Fair to middlin'.'

'Fair to middlin'. An English expression and one that tickles me.'

'You're American?'

'Canadian. My family's business is timber – log conversion, lumber production, grading. Clyde manages the Liverpool sawmill that Papa added to his collection of scalps a couple of years ago.'

'Clyde married the boss's daughter,' Bruce remarked.

'Righty.'

'Is he allowed to forget it?'

'By me or by Papa?'

'By you.'

'Once in a while he feels the sharp end of my shoe. We're in England till Papa is satisfied that the sawmill, which he accepted in settlement of a bad debt, is firmly back on its feet and making money. Then we return home to Quebec and my husband takes his place on the Board. If he's been a good boy, that is.'

'And Estelle will see to it that he has.'

'What else are wives for, Bruce? You say you live in Hurworth, which is the next but one village to ours. We live in Gorman.'

Cameron asked if they liked it.

'Gorman? It'll do. We like Chester, especially the

expensive shops and of course Chester Races. But Liverpool! The Odious City, Aldous Huxley named it. You'll tell me now, Bruce, that you were born and raised there, and in time, as we get to know one another, you'll discover that I'm famous in two continents for saying the wrong thing to the right people. Only last night, I started talking about insanity with a woman whose father, I was told later, had just gone out of his mind.'

'I say I'm from Liverpool because nobody's ever heard of Bayswater,' said Bruce, 'and because the Odious City has produced a list of creative and performing artists that no other place can match, except maybe Dublin. Scousers have a lot to be proud of.'

Estelle had not only heard of Bayswater but had been there. 'We went to look at a house when we first came over. It has an esplanade and faces Liverpool across the Mersey.'

'Check. Does your husband like living in England, Estelle?'

'I've never asked him. We'll always be Canadians. I'm not anti-British, like Papa and Tatou, but I'm not exactly pro- either.'

'Tatou. Your mother?'

'It means armadillo. Her real name is Véronique. We're French Canadians, Roman Catholics, and you'll never hear English spoken at *Les Merles*, even by domestic staff. Clyde was a Protestant from Toronto. He changed for me. His French is fair to middlin', but he only speaks it when he's talking on the telephone with Papa. Our little scamp, Monty, is bilingual. Clyde speaks English with him and I speak French and thus it has been since he burst upon an undeserving world.'

'Some say it's bad for a child's brain.'

'Some talk garbage. How many languages do you speak, Bruce?'

'I'm learning English.'

7

'You show promise.'

'I've thought of learning French and German.'

'Don't think, Bruce. Do.'

'I rather fancy being an export salesman.'

'*Vouloir, c'est pouvoir.*'

'Where there's a will there's a way.'

'*Voilà!*'

'I guessed it from the context.'

Estelle said that languages are a useful adjunct, but a dead end in themselves. She went on: 'If they're all you've got, you can only be a translator, an interpreter or a teacher, which is what I was pre-Monty.'

'What did you teach?'

'French and English. I graduated from Laval University.'

'In Paris?'

'Quebec.'

'With honours?'

'My dear, how else? Before I married, I was Estelle de Champêtre. With a name like that, which can be traced back to the Iron Age, I couldn't be otherwise than first among equals.'

The leader turned in her saddle to call to the riders that they were about to go forward in sitting trot and to be ready to canter at Two Gates.

Intimately, as though to a lover, Estelle said: 'We'll talk again later.'

'Yes, please,' Bruce said, and meant it. Estelle Beaumont knew the right words.

2

In addition to the indoor school (sometimes called the manège) and stabling for some thirty horses and ponies, End Point Riding Centre possessed a retail shop selling riding clothes and accessories, a dormitory block for staff who lived-in and a social club, all of them single-storey and built around the yard in which riders mounted and dismounted.

After leaving Daisy with one of the Centre's voluntary helpers (teenage girls who spent much of their free time there), Cameron went into the club and bought a cup of coffee and a box of matches at the bar. He was joined at his table by the Beaumonts a few minutes later.

Speaking quietly as always, Estelle told her husband to get absent Monty a glass of orange juice and sat down facing Cameron.

'Coffee for you, Estelle?' Clyde prompted.

'Please.'

She fingered soft brown hair away from one eye, inclined her head a little and asked with a smile if Bruce was an agent or a payroll salesman.

He was an agent.

'For three manufacturers. Air rifles, enamelware and camping stoves. Exciting, isn't it? Almost erotic.'

'I guess you're away from home a lot.'

'Monday to Friday. Sporting goods retailers are few and far between. There's one in most towns, two or three in the cities, then a long ride. I've thought once or twice of having my own shop, but I know I'd soon miss the travelling.'

'To say nothing of the challenge, Bruce. Face to face selling like yours calls for nerve and initiative, whereas shopkeeping is dull and passive. CB would make a good shopkeeper.'

'Who's CB?'

'Clyde Beaumont, dear. My husband. He approaches.'

Estelle smiled at him as he placed coffee and orange juice on the table. 'Our new friend,' she said. 'Bruce Cameron.'

Clyde's grip was limp and moist, his smile tentative,

unsure. His wife was clearly the dominant partner. When Monty came in, sniffing back tears as he showed her a grazed wrist, she cut across Clyde's opening words to Cameron, telling him to take the boy to the rest room and wash the wound. 'If a dressing is needed,' she called after him, 'it can wait till we get home.'

'Monty's a handsome lad,' Bruce remarked, feeling that beautiful would be a more appropriate adjective.

'He takes after his father. Slight build, ash blond, bluest of blue eyes. They could both pass for Swiss or Scandinavian.'

'Have you any other children, Estelle?'

She shook her head and sipped her coffee before confessing that she hadn't wanted Monty. She had wanted and still wanted a little girl.

'What's to stop you having one? Perhaps more than one. How old are you? Thirty?'

'Two.'

'You've got bags of time.'

'A woman never knows how much time. Monty's a cry-baby. If I lose patience with him sometimes, it's because he clings to my skirt.'

'He'll grow out of that. What does he like doing, apart from riding and following you around?'

'He knits.'

'*He whats*!'

'Shh! Not even Clyde knows. Monty asked me one day to teach him, so I sat him on my knee and taught him. He keeps his wool and needles with mine, thus to preserve our secret. Knitting, as you may know, was once regarded as among the finer things in life and therefore was enjoyed by males but denied to females. It sedates Monty while I get on with my chores.'

Estelle possessed the brisk adaptability characteristic of her social class. In Canada, at *Les Merles*, servants cooked and cleaned, made beds and waited at table. At

Gorman, in the modest flat she shared with her husband and son, Estelle, at home all day, did everything herself.

Cameron asked what she missed most about Canada. Without hesitation, she answered: 'Oh, the skiing of course. It was my passion and it will be again. The Lawrentian mountains are a skier's paradise, with snow lying for up to twelve weeks in the year. I met lots of boys on the slopes, CB among them.'

'Is he a good skier?'

'Is he a good anything?'

'Here he comes.'

'Complete with Monty, fully repaired and with eyes only for Mama.'

Father and son were similarly dressed in fawn jodhpurs, white tee shirt and brown leather ankle boots. They were holding hands until Monty broke free to skip the rest of the way to his mother's side. His arm went round her shoulders, hers round his waist, and she introduced him to Cameron.

With a nod at the grazed wrist, Cameron asked the boy if it smarted.

'It's nothing,' Estelle decided. Then, to her son: 'Is it, my brave?'

He told Bruce he had tripped and fallen when crossing the yard from the manège to the social club. He had his parents' Canadian accent, an impish smile, an uncomplicated nature.

Sitting down, his father said: 'Monty's accident prone. Aren't you, Monty?'

'He's nothing of the kind,' Estelle retorted.

She turned suddenly to address her husband; and Cameron, over the rim of his cup, saw him flinch. He glanced quickly from man to wife and back again and both of them looked down in momentary confusion.

'I want Bruce to come to our wedding anniversary,' Estelle told Clyde.

11

She asked Cameron if he liked parties.

Monty declared: 'I do.' Still standing, he wriggled contentedly into the crook of his mother's arm, adding: 'Lots of chocolate cake and ice cream. Nunky!'

'Oh, this one's not for little boys,' Estelle chided him, playfully. 'Next Saturday evening, Bruce. Seven thirty onwards. A handful of friends and neighbours. That's all.'

Cameron answered: 'I'd like that' and once again meant what he said. As a rule, he avoided parties, being socially insecure and resentful of time squandered on chit-chat; but the more he listened to Estelle Beaumont, the more he wanted to hear.

'You're not to bring a present,' she told him.

'Is that an order?' he asked, smiling.

'Yes, it is. So do as you're told.'

'Yes, mam.'

'Dress informal,' Clyde said.

'We dress up, Clyde and I, but if you'd rather look as if you've come to fix the boiler, you won't feel out of place,' said Estelle. To her man, she said: 'I've invited Bunty.'

'Plus her husband?'

'Jack won't come.'

'Jack Hazelhurst, teller of tall tales,' Clyde joked, affectionately. 'To listen to Jack, he's done everything short of murder.'

Estelle said: 'He's worked a miracle on Bunty, if what I hear is true. People who remember her when she was plain Bunty Flanagan say she was a sour old maid. I'm pleased for her, pleased for both of them. Jack wasn't far from sleeping rough when they met.'

Cameron lit his pipe, winked at Monty, and watched and listened while the Beaumonts chatted briefly about St Mary's Church at Meadows, where they had attended Mass that morning, and about Estelle's intention of

12

joining Bunty on the roster of voluntary church cleaners.

Estelle was neatly made and of average height and weight, quick and positive in speech and movement, and at her most appealing in black leather riding boots, fawn stretch breeches and navy blue fitted jacket with a black velvet collar. Since puberty, Cameron had been drawn to feminine women in uniform; and here, facing him across the table, was Estelle Beaumont completing his ideal with a starched white shirt and black tie.

Sensing admiration, she met his eyes for a moment, rewarded him with a little smile of understanding and encouragement, and left him wanting nothing so much as to take her in his arms and kiss her lips.

3

Normally, Bruce Cameron looked forward with diminishing enthusiasm to an approaching holiday or social event, so that by the time it arrived he had convinced himself that he would rather stay at home with his records, his fireside reading and his exercise bike. Once there, however, he was usually glad he had made the effort, and this was certainly the case with the Beaumonts' party, where he had the pleasure of seeing Estelle, this time looking delicately feminine in flimsy, high-heeled evening shoes and a cocktail dress of saffron organdie that complemented her brown eyes and hair.

Mockingly, she offered him her hand to kiss before introducing him to her friend, Bunty Hazelhurst. Thereafter, when circulating, she chatted with him more than with anyone else and they smiled at each other now and then between the heads and shoulders of the dozen or so men and women who, talking and drinking to the accompaniment of serene music, filled the sitting room. Otherwise, Bruce spent most of the evening half-listening to Bunty, a complusive talker, while thinking about Estelle and staying alert for glimpses of her.

'So what d'you do for a living?' he asked Bunty, after they had had their highball glasses refilled by Clyde, who was marooned behind a makeshift bar.

'What do I do?' Bunty repeated, on the way back to their armchairs. Her eyes had a twinkle in them. 'You mean when I'm not filming?'

Cameron showed surprise. 'You're an actress?' he questioned.

A less likely one he could scarcely imagine. He had never consciously seen a weasel, but he had decided that this busy little woman with rabbit teeth and a receding chin looked like one and he would henceforth think and speak of her as The Weasel.

'Television,' she replied. 'I've just auditioned for the part of Celia in *Once, Twice and Again*. It's small, but it's work.'

Bruce, watching her with the makings of dislike, said nothing.

She went on: 'No, Mr Cameron. I'm kidding you. Playing the piano at St Mary's Church is the nearest Bunty Hazelhurst gets to showbiz.'

Bruce said: 'I knew a man once named Charles, who tore tickets in half at the Capitol Cinema in Bayswater. He made no secret of the fact that he was a doorman, but always said he was in show business. You've just reminded me of him. I'll have to come to Mass one Sunday. I believe our hosts are regular offenders. Attenders.'

'Worshippers. They come to the twelve o'clock service. Holy Communion. With Monty. Estelle's looking over at us, Brian.'

'Bruce.'

Cameron waved and smiled and boyishly hoped that Estelle was jealous of his being with Bunty.

14

'You'll tell me next your husband's topping the bill at the London Palladium,' he said, unintentionally sounding sarcastic.

'If ever you meet my chap, never mention show business,' Bunty implored. 'Are you old enough to remember Sunny Picket?'

'Only the name. It rhymes with Freddie Bartholomew and Bobby Driscoll.'

'Well, Jack's fate was similar to theirs. They couldn't make the transition from child star to adult actor. Bobby Driscoll was buried in a pauper's grave. Freddie Bartholomew, I think, is still alive but not acting.'

'It must be dreadful to be nobody after being somebody.'

'It's made my chap into one of our country's leading drinkers. I would not say that if Jack didn't say it himself.'

Bunty was taking his photograph out of her bag. Cameron asked how old he was. 'Sixty-one,' she answered. 'Quite frankly, my great fear is that he'll take to drugs, like Bobby Driscoll did, or even kill himself. He sinks into the most awful depression sometimes.'

The photograph showed a tall and intimidating man, unmistakably English, with a fine head, craggy features dominated by a prominent nose and further distinguished by a rattan cigarette holder clamped between his jaws and a monocle on a black silk lanyard.

'Public school?' Cameron muttered, with resentment.

'Just the opposite. Jack is from a humble background, Brian. He was born and raised in Dockside in the East End of London. The Jack Hazelhurst we know today was invented at the start of the 1930s by a benefactor called Clive Valance.'

'I've heard of him. Clive Valance and Faith Winkler. Going back a bit, but not as far back as Henry Irving and Ellen Terry.'

15

'He was an actor-manager. There's now a London theatre named after him, I believe. Well, he spotted my beloved in a school play when Jack was only nine or ten, gave him the name Sunny Picket and the part of the orphan in his stage production of *Once A Policeman* at the Scala Theatre in the West End.'

'How did you meet him?' Bruce asked, handing back the photograph. 'A Londoner and a good few years older than you.'

'Jack is my father, my husband and my child. I saw him for the first time when he came to St Mary's Church for the laying-on of hands.'

'I didn't think that could wean someone off the bottle.'

Clearly miffed, Bunty answered primly: 'Faith can cure anything, Mr Cameron. And it wasn't alcohol that brought Jack into my life. He came seeking relief from spasmodic muscular contraction in his neck, which, when it strikes, presses against the windpipe to create a choking sensation.'

'Couldn't the doctors cure it?'

'My dear, they couldn't even find it. Jack saw his own doctor, then a registrar, then the ear-nose-and-throat specialist himself, had cameras lowered down his throat and was X-rayed. They were looking for a blockage, which is what Jack thought it was at that stage, and of course there wasn't one, so the specialist ended by removing my husband from his clinic after telling him he was wasting NHS time and resources. It was an osteopath who diagnosed it correctly as a soft tissue injury. Jack was going to him for relief from sciatica and just happened to mention his problem for the sake of something to say while the osteopath was jumping on his spine.'

'Then why the laying-on of hands?'

'Because although the osteopath brought him relief through the manipulation of the neck muscles, a cure eluded him and still does. Jack says he's tried everything

16

now short of hanging upside down like a two-toed sloth. Anyhow, Bruce, I must run. Got your name right this time. It's nearly eleven. See you at Mass, I hope.'

'Does Jack join you in your devotions?'

'My chap's a pagan. While I'm praying for his soul, he's playing bowls at the Racquets Club or smoking his fags and reading *The Observer* with a pot of beer in front of him. But he cleans our two rooms and makes our bed, leaving me just the cooking and the shopping. He paints too.'

'Houses?'

'Landscapes. Watercolours. Says they're harder than oils because you can't correct mistakes. Should you ever meet him, remember not to say anything like "Oh, I remember you! Aren't you Sunny Picket?". Quite frankly, Bruce, it demolishes the man.'

'I'll be careful,' Bruce promised, looking round the room and adding: 'Everyone else is leaving too.'

He stood up and emptied his glass as the Beaumonts' telephone rang. He heard Estelle answer in English, then switch to French as he entered the hall, where he found her seated at a crescent-shaped table with a lamp and a white telephone on it. She motioned him to take the chair facing hers and continued in rapid French while blowing a kiss to the last departing guest, whom Clyde saw off the premises before closing the front door and exclaiming: 'Phew!'

To Bruce, with a nod at the telephone, he said: 'The in-laws calling to congratulate us and forgetting the time difference. Quebec is five hours behind Britain. I'll bet they're just about to dress for dinner after an afternoon drive in their monumental Lincoln sedan. Don't go yet, Bruce. The three of us'll have a chat and a nightcap together.'

He started ushering Cameron into the sitting room until checked by Estelle's snapping fingers.

'Papa to speak to you,' she said, giving up her seat to him and watching his face.

Cameron stood by while Estelle, seeming to forget his presence, listened intently to Clyde's staggering about in French as he attempted answers to Louis de Champêtre's questions about the week's business at the Liverpool sawmill. He was clearly not enjoying the experience, but his wife, standing over him with arms folded under her bust, fingers twitching and one knee a little forward inside her dress, unashamedly was, watching him in silence and without sympathy.

Chapter Two

The more Bruce Cameron thought about Estelle, the more attractive she became. He wanted to see her, talk about her, hear about her; and the opportunity to do all three arrived sooner than expected. Shortly after his riding lesson at End Point on the Friday evening following the anniversary party, he opened the front door of his bungalow in Hurworth to find Clyde Beaumont smiling at him and asking if he would like to have a drink with him. He suggested they go in his car, a sage-green Jensen, to Meadows, the village midway between Hurworth and Gorman, and to the Freemason's Arms, a name which provided his excuse for asking if his companion was a Mason.

Cameron took his pipe from between his teeth and his smile was almost a leer.

'You're not supposed to ask that question,' he pointed out.

'Which tells me you are,' Clyde deduced. 'Estelle thinks it would be a good idea if I joined.'

'Just like that,' Bruce said, with a snap of his fingers.

'She has this theory, you know, that if a man doesn't get away from women occasionally, he becomes one.'

'Nobody is automatically excluded from Freemasonry, Clyde, but I think your Faith forbids you to join. If you

19

don't mind my saying so, it's another example of the Vatican seeking to control the thoughts and actions of the faithful.'

'Say whatever you like to me, Bruce. I'm a convert. I attend divine offices, as Estelle has started calling them – Bunty's term for what we know as church services – partly to keep the peace and partly as an example to Monty.'

Emboldened, Cameron said: 'Roman Catholicism is a mirror image of Marxist Communism, which is why the Vatican supported the Nazis and turned a blind eye to the persecution and then the extermination of the Jews. Jews and Communists were one and the same to Hitler, just as they were to Pope Pius the Twelfth, who is still called by some Hitler's Pope. Eichmann, his family and other SS leaders escaped capture by the Allies thanks to the German Bishop of Rome, who slipped them Vatican passports.'

Clyde wasn't interested. He asked if Masons were branded with hot irons, adding: 'My wife says they are, but I don't know where she got it from.'

'Don't believe it. Listen! There's nothing sinister in Freemasonry and nothing subversive either. Every Mason takes an oath of allegiance to the Monarch as well as to the Government of the day, whether or not he supports them.'

'Masons look after themselves though, don't they?'

'In what way?'

'In every way. I heard a programme about them on my car radio the other day and one of the panel described them as sleek, selfish and well-fed.'

'We enjoy dining together, if that's what he meant by well-fed. So far from being selfish, we contribute to several charities, by no means all of them Masonic. Whoever it was spouting on your radio had probably never entered a Lodge in his life.'

'It was a woman. When I told Estelle, she said she couldn't possibly know what she was talking about because women aren't allowed to become Masons.'

'Well, that's wrong too. There are women's Lodges, at any rate here in Britain, but they're not recognised by Grand Lodge. Why women want to imitate men beats me, but they're doing it more and more,' Cameron lamented. 'We hear them pressing for access to men's clubs and societies, but I haven't heard of men beating on the door of the Mothers' Union or the Women's Institute.'

'Estelle suggested I ask you about it, Bruce. I hope you don't mind.'

'It's good to have the chance to blow away some of the crazy notions people have about the Order. Our self-imposed silence breeds mistrust and misunderstanding. Those who know don't speak: those who speak don't know. I forget who said that, but I like it because it's true. Another pint of Reklaw's celebrated bitter, Clyde?'

'It's my round.'

'I didn't like to say. Incidentally, I'm amused by Estelle's habit of calling you CB,' Bruce remarked. 'Perhaps one day she'll turn it round and call me BC.'

Clyde gave him the nervous, ingratiating smile that seldom left his face and said his wife called him CB when she was pleased with him: otherwise, he was Dumbell or Beaumont. Getting up, he muttered, still with his flickering smile: 'You're a wise judge to stay single, Bruce.'

Cameron watched him while he awaited service at the crowded bar and wondered what had induced Estelle to choose this self-effacing man in preference to those other suitors she had mentioned. Clyde was lower class, like Cameron, but colourless and easily managed, whereas Bruce was virile, assertive and unquestionably handsome. Estelle obviously left Clyde undisturbed regarding

21

his appearance; since his Attaboy trilby, Swallow macintosh and Tootal tie had all passed away with the advent of motoring-for-all. Bruce could picture him before his marriage, living contentedly at home with Mother and Father, padding off to a desk job on splayed feet, like an old waiter, with a smile and a nod for all who knew him, a packed lunch in his brief case and the *Toronto Star* to read on the train. At thirty-five, he was five years younger than Bruce, but five years older in aspect and temperament.

Returning to the table with fresh pints, he said: 'Estelle says to bring you home after this for a bite of supper – just cheese and biscuits and a cup of coffee.'

'Thanks, Clyde. You're lucky to have her, you know.'

'She likes you. Don't tell her I said this, but she's changed the time of our Sunday hack to coincide with yours.'

'She told me she was doing it because of a change in the time of Monty's lesson in the manège.'

'Not so. She thought it would be nice to ride with you because you're so much alone, what with your job and living by yourself.'

'That's very kind.'

'No need to mention it to her,' Clyde cautioned. 'Estelle can be the sweetest woman in the world, but never get on the wrong end of her temper. Phew! Estelle's the only child of an old and autocratic family. She's used to wealth and obedience. She's Old Isoscelys all over again.'

Amused, Bruce said: 'Isoscelys is a triangle with two sides of equal length. At least, it was when I went to school.'

'I understand it still is; but it's also Monty's name for his grandfather, Louis de Champêtre, the man I spoke to in French – or tried to – after our little party.'

'By my standards, CB, you won a weekend for two in Blackpool.'

'The old devil speaks English as easily as you do. He is expert at wrong-footing me and so is Estelle. Both are quick thinkers, which I am not, with the family business coming first, second and third. My wife, Bruce, not me, is the sawmill manager.'

2

Back at the Beaumonts' flat in Gorman, talking together within range of the gas fire, Estelle presently brought the conversation round to Freemasonry; but when Clyde told her that the Pope discourages Catholics from becoming Masons, she briskly resumed her knitting and said that in that case the matter was closed.

'I just thought membership might benefit CB in business,' she told Cameron.

She crossed one thigh over the other and plucked at the hem of her knee-length skirt. It was a habit of hers, Bruce would presently notice, and an indication that she was displeased.

He explained: 'The giving or receiving of favours is strictly taboo in Masonry. A brother caught breaking the code would be invited to resign from his Lodge.'

'Bruce says Masons never declare themselves except to other Masons and sometimes not even then,' Clyde said. 'He knows of a family where the two sons, married and living at separate addresses, belong to different Lodges and neither of them knows the other is a Mason.'

Cameron went on to say that Masonry does a lot of good and no harm at all. 'If I had to sum it up in two words, I'd call it agreeable nonsense. The ranking order within a Lodge confers distinction, however spurious, on men who otherwise have none. Men like me. They clank around in worthless regalia, exchanging passwords and paying one another vast compliments on having memorised half a

23

page of ritual. It's all an elaborate and enjoyable extention of gang-hut secrecy and comradeship.'

'Your talk is often bookish,' Estelle remarked. 'Did you go to college, Bruce? I've heard of a very good one in the Odious City with a name like Mariner's.'

Tickled, her husband said: 'Alumni are called Ancient Mariners. Cute, isn't it? My deputy at the mill is one.'

'I went to Bayswater Grammar School,' Bruce said. 'Gone now. It was originally a choir school, founded in the reign of the first Elizabeth and closed in the reign of the second.'

Clyde sneezed twice, making Estelle smile at him and say to Cameron: '*C'est toujours le double chez lui*. Did you learn French, Bruce?'

'Safer to say I fought it, as I did Shakespeare and similar horrors.'

'And what did you do after you left?' Estelle asked.

'I went to Cammell Laird's shipyard and served a five-year apprenticeship as a marine engineer,' Bruce answered.

He had been a serious though not solemn young man, attending night school as an obligatory part of his apprenticeship while at the same time broadening his education, though not his outlook, with a careful study of the political writings of Bernard Shaw and H.G.Wells. Among the few novels he had read in his lifetime was *The New Machiavelli*. His vision remained one of narrow, doctrinaire Socialism until, after serving as a borough councillor and failing to be adopted as a parliamentary candidate, he had experienced a gradual change of attitude and aspirations when in his early thirties. The fiery speaker, the trade union activist quick with his fists, and the persistent critic of the Monarchy had slowly mellowed into the conforming businessman who now told the Beaumonts that his letters to the Queen had brought him to the attention of the Special Branch.

'You must tell us the story one day,' Estelle said, with only polite interest. 'For the moment, just say what is special about the branch. I don't think we have one in Canada, have we, Clyde?'

He answered: 'Oh, I should think we have, lurking here and there in plain clothes and unmarked cars, watching and listening. Do you remember that case in Winnipeg a few years ago, when a strike leader was waylaid and badly beaten by three masked men? I gave a lift to a military policeman shortly thereafter and I said to him *"The culprits still haven't been found, have they?"* and he said *"No, and they never will be"*. I said *"What does that mean?"*. He said *"What do you think it means?"*. *"Oh"* I said, *"things like that don't happen here"*. *"Don't they?"* he said, turning to look at me. *"Don't they? Don't you kid yourself"*.'

'The Special Branch protects our Royal Family,' Cameron explained. 'Along with all their other indulgences and extravagances, it's financed by the taxpayer – by you and me, in other words.'

To his wife, Clyde said: 'Old Isoscelys should hear this, Estelle. It might bring the shadow of a smile to his thin lips. He calls the Royal Family the last of the great feudal monarchies, Bruce, stuffing itself off gold plate while the rest of us bow and curtsy to it.'

'Papa wants Prime Minister Thatcher to sell the Family to the Americans as part of her privatisation programme,' Estelle revealed. 'Clyde, fetch the whisky for our guest. The single malt. None for you though. You've got to drive him home.'

Bruce said he could call a taxi.

'You could, but you're not going to,' said Estelle, as her husband left the room. She liked looking at Cameron. 'What do you do at weekends, aside from the Sunday hack?'

'I have my sewing.'

25

'It's my guess you clean house and do the week's marketing, with maybe a visit to the laundrette.'

'Tomorrow, Saturday, I'll play squash in Chester, then go to Dixie Dean's for a pot of beer and a sandwich. Clerical work in the pm. Sunday morning I'm at the clay shoot. In Canada, you probably call it skeet shooting. Clay discs are sent aloft from a spring-device known as a trap and the man who shatters the lowest number of discs buys the beer.'

'I've heard them cracking away from Bunty Hazelhurst's. She and Jack live in Meadows, in a house opposite St Mary's Church,' said Estelle.

'I like your dog,' Bruce said, nodding over his pipe at Fiver, who was stretched out and asleep on the hearthrug. 'A dog of uncertain lineage, but all the more interesting for that and probably all the more loving.'

'He's very loyal. Have you tried fox hunting?' Estelle asked. 'No? Why not try it with me? You know the Master of the Hermitage Hunt. You met him at our party.'

'Major Shobbrook.'

'Righty. He's invited us, CB and me, to any Wednesday Meet, but CB can't manage midweek. You could ride Countess, his horse. Think about it.'

Clyde returned with The Glenlivet, apologising for the delay and explaining that the bottle had not been in its usual place.

'My fault,' said Estelle. 'I gave Jack a shot when he was here with Bunty for the church coffee morning and suffering from re-entry symptoms after a boozy night.'

Cameron asked how the Beaumonts' dog had come to be called Fiver.

'That's what we paid for him,' Clyde explained.

Estelle took up the story. 'My little cry-baby wanted a pet and I don't like cats – too much like women – so we took him to the Dogs' Home. Cats are lazy little tykes. I mean they don't do anything, do they, except eat, sleep and reproduce? They don't guide the blind, sniff-out explosives, assist with arrests, guard property, locate people buried under rubble ... They're as sybaritic and parasitic as your Royal Family.'

'What a sight it was, that Dogs' Home!' Clyde exclaimed. 'Phew! We'd never seen one before, had we, Estelle? There must have been fifteen poor, abandoned wretches in a big cage, jumping up and barking at us and frantic to have a new owner. Fiver, as we decided to call him, was alone and silent and utterly forlorn, slumped in a corner and looking as though he had lost all hope of ever being rescued.'

'It was a warm day, but he was shivering,' Estelle went on. 'I nursed him in my lap and tickled his ears on the drive back here and told him we were going to give him a good home with his own bed and lots to eat and Monty would walk him every day. We waited two weeks before bathing him, thinking it might be an unsettling experience. He's one of the family now.'

Cameron nodded his approval and sipped his whisky and heard from Clyde that Monty was teaching Fiver to perform tricks and memorise words. 'English or French?' he asked.

'English. Somehow, it seemed more natural,' Estelle answered. 'Listening to Monty made me think how surprising it is that we've all agreed on the meaning of words. All over the English-speaking world, for example, a chair is a chair and a desk is a desk; whereas, human nature being so often capricious, even perverse, you would expect pockets of resistance, with some people refusing to conform, just as certain areas of Britain – Oxford among them – stubbornly clung to local time instead of adopting Greenwich Time until the spread of the railroads and later of broadcasting brought them round to standardisation.'

Smiling at his wife, Clyde told her she should write a

monograph on the subject and call it *When And Where Is A Chair Not A Chair*?

'Or get Monty to write it,' Bruce suggested. 'He's a smart lad for his age. Has he decided what he wants to be yet or is it still too early?'

'I don't think Monty wants to be anything except his mother's extra pair of hands,' said Clyde. 'I've never known a boy so content to be indoors. Never.'

'How many have you known?' Estelle countered, sharply, plucking at the hem of her skirt.

'When I was his age, you couldn't keep me in the house,' Clyde elaborated. 'I was out there with the other kids, playing baseball, swimming, fishing the stream in back of the house, getting into mischief. What d'you say we buy him a bike, Estelle, and I'll teach him to ride?'

'We may be back home in Canada before the end of the year. It only needs a word from Papa. You'd be better employed thinking up ways of attracting new business than teaching your son to ride a pushbike.'

Cameron, with a glance at his watch, asked if he might use the bathroom. When he came out of it, the passage light had been switched off and Estelle Beaumont was waiting in shadow for him. She stepped into his arms and hard, hungry kissing began.

'Clyde ...' Bruce murmured, when they paused for breath.

'He knows better than to interfere,' Estelle replied, her cheek cool against Cameron's, her splayed fingers exploring his shoulders.

She told his ear that she had a feline interest in the interiors of other people's homes and asked when it would be convenient to see his.

3

She came in her car when Clyde was at the mill and
Bruce was taking an afternoon off. On her way from
Gorman, passing through Meadows, she had deposited
her little cry-baby at End Point Riding Centre.

'No school today?' Bruce asked, as she entered his
bungalow. 'Are the little darlings on holiday yet again? I
haven't seen The Terrible Trio dancing round a football
in front of the lounge windows as yet, but I'm sure they
haven't forgotten me. I'd feel deprived if they had.'

'I teach Monty at home. You don't like children, do
you?' Estelle chided him, and playfully repeated her
earlier charge that he was a selfish old bachelor.

Bruce replied: 'I don't mind girls, but lads are an
infernal nuisance from the moment they draw breath.
Monty excepted. Is he bobbing up and down in the
manège?'

'No. He's working. His choice. I said he could go
there today as a reward for getting his sums right this
morning.'

'Aren't you a marvel? You think of everything.'

'He likes working there and it gets him out of the
apartment and among people, albeit only women and
girls. He mucks-out and cleans tack and helps with
grooming. Show me this famous exercise parlour of
yours. That's the only reason I'm here.'

Cameron led the way through his kitchen and into the
full-width conservatory, where weights, a chest expander
and a rowing machine kept company with an exercise
bike on a floor close-fitted with fawn coconut matting.

'We should have a bike like that at Gorman,' Estelle
said. 'If I could pick one up cheaply, the three of us
could use it. As it is, we're not getting enough exercise.
CB doesn't take any at all.'

'I could get a new one for you at cost price.'

'Would that be cheaper than buying one second hand?'

'Probably about the same. Leave it with me.'

'Righty. What time is it?'

Cameron found Estelle's hand.

'Time you saw the rest of the bungalow,' he answered. 'Come! This is the kitchen, where I cook my meals and eat them and wash up afterwards. Weekends only, of course.'

'Beware of hotel food. It's rich in fats and sugars. Unfortunately, they are what give taste to food.'

'I'm pretty careful what I eat, without being one of these freaks who stick to a diet of carrot juice and bread baked with sawdust and iron filings. Plenty of fresh fruit and exercise to keep diabetes at bay.'

'Oh, my poor mother is cursed with it. Her own fault, she's the first to admit. A lifetime of virtual inactivity and nowadays too much sitting watching television, playing contract and waiting for the parlourmaid to appear in the doorway and say "*Madame est servie*".'

Cameron said that when away from home he had a swim or a workout most evenings before dinner and later a glass of whisky before bed. He made regular use of the leisure centres, health clubs and gymnasiums located here and there on his territory.

'You use this as your office,' Estelle announced, pausing at the threshold of the smallest of the three bedrooms. 'I note the desk, the telephone, and the tax demand on your pink blotter. How neat and soldierly you are! Males tend to drop everything where they finish using it. My thoughts go to CB, to the towel askew on its rail and the lavatory seat yawning at me as I enter the bathroom.'

'There's a story to my tax demand,' Bruce said.

'I feared there might be.'

'The Inland Revenue questioned the figure I gave for private milage, suggesting I agree to a higher one. I said that to do so would be to make a false declaration and I was sure they weren't asking me to do that. A stunned silence followed. Then, after about three weeks, came a notice saying they felt the higher figure was more realistic and therefore I would be assessed on it. What's known, Estelle, as pulling rank. Come and see my bedroom.'

'No time, darling, so please return my hand to its rightful owner.'

'This won't take a minute, Estelle. I promise.'

'Well, only a minute, then I must sprout wings. I imagine your bedroom is full of photos of girls and aeroplanes and strewn with the entrails of an old motor cycle.'

It wasn't. But it did contain a double divan bed and soft warmth convected by a fan heater.

'I suppose you think you're going to seduce me,' Estelle murmured, still holding Cameron's hand.

'You must have gipsy blood,' he replied.

He clasped her in his arms and they kissed and kissed until she told him he was a very naughty boy.

'Does that mean you're going to spank me?' he prompted, almost crooning the words.

Into his ear, she said: 'Only little boys get spanked, like my cry-baby and the ones I taught in Canada. I caned the bigger boys. How would you like that, my toad?'

Cameron affected a shudder and said 'God forbid!', but Estelle's words had made him light-headed, shortening his breath and stiffening his erection. Roused in her turn by the feel of it against her, Estelle, squirming into it, ended more kissing with 'Why don't you undress me? I've always had trouble with zips. I sometimes think they were invented to spite and frustrate me.'

On his knees in front of her and loving the position, Bruce removed her navy leather shoes and stood them together on their high heels. Then, while she smiled down into his black eyes, he took off her knee-length skirt and her white tunic with blue piping at the cuffs and revers. He was to discover that this combination of silk slip, short-sleeved tunic, plain navy skirt and matching court shoes was Estelle's customary attire. He would find out too that the absence of a bra was not peculiar to their first love-making. She never needed one.

'You have small feet,' she observed, stripped now to the nylons and suspender belt that she would retain. Hands on hips, she was watching Cameron remove his trainers and socks. 'Does that mean over here what it means in Canada?'

'Suck it and see.'

'I shall do no such thing. I'll undress you though.'

Estelle set to work.

'Pants down first, then the underpants, white and sexless. If you were my husband, I'd make you wear coloured boxer shorts. Shirt next, singlet after that and bingo! He's ready for action.'

The lovers kissed in each other's arms; then Estelle, rubbing noses, inhaled the scent of his body and made murmuring sounds of appreciation.

'You're all man, aren't you?' she breathed, caressing his naked shoulders. 'All beef and no fat. Tumtum flat as a board.'

'I'd like to be taller.'

'Than? '

'Five feet eight.'

'But you're in proportion. You've got a squared-off look and a waist and hips some women would like to have. Think I'll call you Tarzan.'

Bruce scooped her up in his arms, carrying her to his bed while she, with both arms round his neck, kicked her legs and squealed her protest and demanded to know what he was doing to her. In bed, cleaving to him, she whispered endearments and asked wistfully if he could give her a little girl.

'What would your husband say?'

'He'd think she was his.'

'And you'd let him?'

'Sure. '

'So much for your Faith.'

'Special dispensation.'

'Not to mention your integrity.'

'You don't know how desperate a woman can become. Let's find out how potent your love-juice is.'

Estelle's small, experienced hand went to work, stroking and rubbing while Bruce kissed her ears, lips, eyelids and neck, fondling her rosebuds, stimulating her clitoris. Soon her technique and dedication raised him to a state of exaltation he had never before attained. Hot spurts of joy obliterated the distaste he sometimes felt for the human body.

They rested, temporarily satiated, in each other's arms, kissing when not talking.

Bruce asked: 'Are you happy with CB?'

'I haven't come here to talk about my husband.'

'What's he like in bed?'

'Fair to middlin'. I make him come even when he pleads tiredness. I want that little girl, Bruce, I want her bad and the clock doesn't stop ticking. Clyde has never been otherwise than a means to an end. I don't pretend I ever loved him and he's never said he loves me. I've wanted children ever since I was a schoolgirl. I told myself I'd be married by age twenty-one and married I was.'

Cameron had already decided that Estelle de Champêtre had married Clyde Beaumont and not the other way round. He guessed accurately that her domineering nature had frightened off two or three suitors before she found the one who allowed himself to be led into matrimony.

'If I hadn't hoisted Dumbell out of his rut, he'd have remained a shipping clerk till the day he received his Teasmade,' she muttered. 'When I brought him home to be introduced, Papa and Tatou stared at him as if I'd found him under a stone. They fought the marriage tooth and claw until it was obvious my mind was made up.'

Clyde moved into *Les Merles* and Louis de Champêtre, adapting unwillingly to the situation, gave him a management position in the family business after sending him to Harvard Business School on a residential course. Every weekend for six months, Clyde brought his work home to be read by his wife, who wanted to be sure Papa was getting value for his money.

Estelle started playing with Cameron.

'Their only daughter being married to a clerk was more than my parents could swallow,' she explained. 'They gradually became resigned to CB – you can't go on excluding a man who tries so hard to please – but he remains an intruder. Tatou still refers to him as *'ton garçon de café'*. With everyone speaking French at home, I mostly had to interpret if Clyde was in the room. It was that or leave him tickling the cat.'

It was not difficult to picture Estelle wilfully isolating him from time to time as punishment for some minor misdemeanour, as a reminder of his lowly place in the family or to show her contempt for a man who allowed her to scold and order him about in the presence of others.

Cameron said: 'Would you really let him believe your baby was his when you knew she was mine?'

'How would I know she was yours and not his?'

'If you guessed she was mine – and I'm sure a woman has a pretty shrewd idea about such things – would you marry me, Estelle?'

'Wow! That came straight from outer space.'

'Would you?'

34

'I can't divorce.'

'Yet another manipulation of your Faith. Adultery, yes; divorce, no. If I knew you better and at the risk of having my face slapped—'

'Go on. I'm good at that.'

'—I'd say that Roman Catholicism is the most cynical, selfish and cowardly of all the Christian denominations.'

'Wait till you know me better, then I'll slap your face. Hard. Let's make delicious love one more time and I want you to pump your hardest and think girl, girl, girl. You need a little tuition, by the way, and more practice.'

'Who better to teach me than a teacher?'

They sank into kissing and fondling.

'I do love that little nose of yours,' Bruce whispered. 'I'm something of a connoisseur where noses are concerned.'

'I'm not parting with it. In fact, I'm taking it with me in about twenty minutes' time.'

'It's so slim, so delicately carved, and it has a sheen, you know, as if the bone was showing through. Don't ever powder it, will you?'

The lovers fell silent after Estelle had murmured that if she were late calling to collect Monty, she would find him in tears.

Chapter Three

Friday evenings with Clyde at the Freemason's Arms, a fireside supper afterwards at the Beaumonts' flat, and fevered love-making at Cameron's bungalow became routine. On his birthday, Bruce took the couple to dinner at the Grosvenor Hotel in the heart of Chester – a new experience for them and a pleasant one. He felt it was the least he could do in return for their hospitality.

Estelle drove, using her red Metro rather than her husband's Jensen, thereby allowing the men to drink more than was good for them. It didn't surprise Cameron to learn in the course of the evening that it was Estelle who bought and sold their cars, never keeping them longer than eighteen months. Despite her considerable means, the cars she bought were always second-hand, and Bruce would one day discover that she was a hard though not aggressive bargainer. Estelle invested in quality, as was evident in the beautiful clothes she wore that evening, but she kept a careful watch on day-to-day expenditure.

The trio returned to the Beaumonts' apartment shortly after ten o'clock. On her way to the kitchen to make coffee, Estelle told Monty to go to bed, while Bruce and Clyde settled contentedly into armchairs.

'Ah, why can't I stay up?' the boy pleaded.

'Because I say you can't and adults' wishes take precedence over children's,' Estelle told him. 'Now run along. It's way past your bedtime.'

Monty looked beseechingly at the men, but only for a moment. He knew who gave the orders and he followed her, grizzling, into the kitchen. Bruce heard her ask how he had spent the evening. His reply was inaudible.

Clyde said: 'This is the first time we've left him alone after dark. Estelle suggested asking Bunty Hazelhurst to sit with him, but Monty said he'd be okay on his own.'

Bruce wondered if he had been knitting, what sort of items he knitted (egg-cosies came to mind) and what he did with them when they were finished.

'Estelle tells me you call this block of flats Oildrum Court,' he said to CB. He smiled. 'Boom, boom, boom.'

'Stud walls. Hollow inside. No soundproofing,' Clyde explained. 'You must have noticed. We go to bed with the people upstairs and get up with the people downstairs.'

'I've heard them setting the table. Heard the spoons tinkling into the saucers.'

'That's not the only tinkling you'll hear, Bruce. Wait till the old boy overhead drains his bladder before going to bed. Sometimes he treats us to sound effects as well. You won't credit this, but if next door's telephone rings we go to answer ours.'

'Well, I can credit it because I lived in a flat in Bayswater with my sister and her husband after our mother and father died. Noise was a permanent problem, so when Joan and Ray emigrated to Australia I scouted round for a detached bungalow and landed, as you know, in Hurworth – in Sunnyside Gardens Estate to be precise.'

'In the County Palatine of Chester,' Clyde said, amused by the novelty of the title. 'My Ancient Mariner assistant at the sawmill tells me there are two Counties

37

Palatine in Britain, the other one being the County Palatine of Lancaster.'

'Righty, as Estelle would say. Long ago, a County Palatine was governed by an earl, who had sovereign powers of life and death over the inhabitants. Each county was known by the name of its county town, so Chester for Cheshire and Lancaster for Lancashire. Don't you wonder, Clyde, how you've survived as long as you have without knowing that? Incidentally I have the ideal neighbour in Hurworth. Mrs Ford. If we are unlucky, we see each other once a year. But it's a shame about this place of yours, because you're high up in the world and with a splendid view.'

'Jack Hazelhurst, Bunty's tosspot husband, wants to paint it. Have you seen any of his pictures, Bruce? He's quite good, you know.'

'Despite the shakes,' said Estelle, returning with coffee things on a tray and her son hard on her heels. 'Say goodnight to Daddy and Mr Cameron, Monty, then off to bed with you. I'll be along to tuck you in presently.'

Clyde said, once the boy was out of earshot: 'Isn't it time, Estelle, you cut this goodnight kiss ritual? And isn't it time you put him into long trousers instead of keeping him trussed into the briefest and tightest of short pants?'

Estelle said she would decide when it was time. 'As to the kiss, if I forget he wets the bed. And gets a smacking.'

'Over your knee?' Cameron suggested, lighting his pipe and savouring the words.

'I have accommodating thighs, Bruce,' she told him, quietly.

He answered that hers were as long as Bunty's were short.

'You've noticed,' she said.

38

Clyde chuckled wickedly.

'Bunty's got duck's disease. Her ass is too near the ground,' he claimed.

He wanted to know if Cameron found her attractive. Bruce shook his head, remarking that The Weasel had a nose shaped like one half of a wishbone. Welcoming this chance to criticise a woman he considered insincere and untrustworthy, he went on to say that he could readily imagine her nostrils twitching like those of a rat scenting something to eat.

Crossing one thigh over the other and plucking at her skirt, Estelle replied coldly that a person's exterior was of no importance. She continued: 'If you knew the half of what Bunty does for St Mary's Church and the care she lavishes on her husband, you'd have only praise for her. Bunty and Jack Hazelhurst were the first to befriend us when we settled in Gorman.'

Cameron was unrelenting.

'Viewed from the rear, she looks like a dog walking on its hind legs,' he said.

Clyde started laughing. He shared Bruce's mistrust of Bunty and didn't welcome her subtle influence over his wife.

'She has a long torso and short legs with a blob of bottom in between,' he stated.

'Bunty wears the wrong clothes,' Estelle pointed out, firmly in defence of her. 'That's all that's the matter.'

'Bunty has only one outfit,' Clyde chortled. 'That greasy grey two-piece with a jacket that's more like a truncated overcoat.'

'Blame Jack for that. She's out earning money while he stays home doing the washing and ironing and waiting for the Racquets Club to open,' said Estelle. Rising, she added: 'I'd better give my little cherub his kiss before he starts calling out to ask if I'm all right.'

'A kiss at his age!' Clyde exclaimed, scornfully, when

Estelle was out of the room. 'He'll be wanting to knit next.'

Bruce said nothing, so Clyde went on with: 'I'm concerned about the boy. He doesn't want a train set, doesn't want a skate board, won't come with me to see a football match ... Just wants his mother all the time, the more so when she doesn't want him.'

'He'll grow out of it.'

'And I don't like what he's doing at End Point either. It's sickly. He's persuaded his mother to let him spend Saturday afternoons there, filling buckets and haynets. I can understand girls wanting to care for animals, but boys ... What did you do when you were Monty's age, Bruce?'

'Swam in the sea in all weathers, went for bike rides with my pal, did a little rowing on West Float ...'

'Well, that's what I mean.'

'Once I started my apprenticeship, I used to cross to Liverpool on the ferry for the Friday night fights at Peterkin's Gym. Sometimes I watched, sometimes I went five rounds with an instructor.'

'Any family, Bruce? Apart from Joan? Brothers?'

'Just Joan. She practically brought me up after Mother and Father were killed.'

'Estelle should let Monty go to school,' Clyde said, 'where he'd mix with other boys.'

'Has he asked to be sent?'

Clyde shook his head slowly and sadly, then sipped his coffee as sounds reached them from the flat above.

'The old boy's off to kip,' he announced, gleefully. 'Hear him tinkling? Chances are, Bruce, he'll release a rich, liberating fart.'

'Where do I take cover?'

'Wow! Hear it?' CB cried, in triumph.

'I'd have to be on Mars not to. I call that a block-buster.'

'You've missed the fun, Estelle,' Clyde declared, as his wife came back into the room. 'Old Joe upstairs has just treated us to a rip-snorter.'

Colouring slightly, Estelle glanced warily at Cameron, then gave her husband a look that would have set his buttocks twitching had he been sober.

'You've had too much to drink,' she told him, ominously, and held his gaze for a moment before sitting down and telling Bruce that the apartment was only rented.

'It's better than sleeping in the park, but only just,' she admitted. 'Look at the furniture. I should guess it was stolen from a bonfire the night before the blaze.'

The carpet was a chenille – thin, cheap and gaudy – and its surrounds were liver-coloured thermoplastic tiles. On it stood a three-piece cottage suite with beech arms and frames, its rubber seating and backrests upholstered in brown cotton flecked with orange and gold. The flock wallpaper, the standard lamp, the high-gloss coffee table and the hissing gas fire were likewise the landlord's choice. Only the colour television, rarely used, belonged to the Beaumonts.

'I'd be frightened to turn my back on those curtains,' Bruce joked. 'It's the first time I've seen them closed and in their full glory.'

'Big black dragons on a gold ground,' said Clyde. 'Chosen by a blind man in a power blackout.'

Estelle nearly said: 'All rather different from Hurworth', but checked herself in time to change the location to *Les Merles*.

'Nice name, that,' Cameron remarked, taking the pipe from between his teeth.

'It's French for The Blackbirds,' Clyde said, approvingly. 'A lovely name for a lovely old villa.' He turned, smiling, to his wife. 'You miss your real home, Estelle, yet you never complain.'

41

Les Merles was long and low. The floors throughout were of Tasmanian oak; the stairs, doors and cupboards of mountain ash from Victoria; the roof of Canadian cedar shingles. The rooms were centrally heated in winter and cooled in summer by ceiling fans. Servants had their separate entrance, with stairs leading up to the mansard.

'The furniture and oil paintings are all antique and came over from France with my ancestors,' Estelle revealed. 'I always liked the carpets – handmade to order, plain cream with floral clusters in the corners.'

Clyde said: 'Simple country boy that I am, I used to think washed Chinese simply meant the carpet had been cleaned. Not so.'

'It means it was washed at the factory with a glycerine solution to soften the colours,' Estelle told Bruce. She went on: '*Les de Champêtre* came originally from the Auvergne, where they had *une propriété foncière* – what you call over here a landed estate. Papa is the last of the line. His brother was killed in the Second World War.'

'It's time I got from under your feet,' said Bruce. 'If you'll let me use your phone, I'll ring for a taxi.'

But once again his hostess wouldn't hear of it. She would drive him the few miles to Hurworth.

'I hope you both realise that you sounded like catty schoolgirls when you were pulling Bunty's plaits just now,' she said. She slid her hands into leather gloves and added: 'You ought to be ashamed of yourselves, both of you. Come along, Bruce. We'll leave CB to wash the dishes by way of penance.'

Looking back on his way out of the room, Bruce said: 'See you on Friday, Clyde, at the Freemason's.'

'If I let him go,' said Estelle.

In her car, his temperature raised by those last words, Cameron took her in his arms and covered her face and neck with kisses.

The two men looked forward to each other's company on Friday evenings. The working week was over. They could relax with their beer and make their contribution to the surrounding buzz of conversation. With no commitments and nobody to consult, Cameron was invariably there on the dot of eight o'clock, sitting by the fire in the bar and ready to get up and buy Clyde a pint as soon as his kind and apologetic face came round the door.

'Phew!' he began, raising his glass to Bruce before drinking. 'I need this, believe me! You're not married. I'm tempted to say stay that way. You can only guess at what a relief it is to get away from it all for a couple of hours. Estelle has to know every detail of what's happening at the mill.'

Bruce envied him his marriage to her, but recognised it didn't bring CB the pleasure that Bruce believed it would bring him. Clyde was nervous and often miserable under her scrutiny, never knowing the minute when she would make him squirm. 'I have to be very careful what I say,' he confessed, with his flickering smile. He was frightened of her tongue and, Bruce suspected, of her hands as well. He believed she let him go drinking partly because she wanted Bruce's company afterwards and partly because a brief respite would make the sting of her domination that bit sharper.

Cameron had seen a change in Clyde even in the few months of their association. His almost constant smile – a partial baring of the front upper teeth – had become sicklier, more faltering, and his slight stoop a little more pronounced, as though in anticipation of the whip. He blinked a lot and occasionally his cheek twitched. He was often preoccupied, dwelling, it seemed to Bruce, on disturbing thoughts. Clyde was a good man who needed a homely wife, a man whom Nature had designed to live in a backwater. The job he had been given was too big for him and made no easier by Estelle's 'Don't dare let Papa down', uttered more than once in Cameron's presence. She had her husband on the point of a skewer; and sometimes, knitting with one leg crossed over the other, she would allow herself the cold pleasure of making him writhe.

'I just feel I'd like to be a hobo,' he muttered, looking ahead at nothing and forcing a chuckle. 'There should be more to life than work, Bruce, and then an inquest over dinner.'

'Not every night, surely?'

'Oh, yes. I can send out for a packet of tea or have the windows washed without asking her, but I can't order stationery without shopping round for the best price. She checks all the bills before I pay them, including the telephone account, then she reports to Old Isoscelys at the weekend in rapid, idiomatic French, which means I can't always figure out what they're saying about me.'

'The pressure will be off once you're back in Canada, Clyde.'

'Not so. It'll be worse, because then I'll have both of them to contend with. Estelle is her father's understudy, and at his death she'll replace him. It's all part of a plan, Bruce. Just as Fiver has been taught tricks by Monty, I'm being taught enough to play the chief executive; but in reality I'll be the puppet of the woman who pulls the strings.'

'I don't know how you stand it,' Bruce said, wishing himself in Clyde's place.

'I don't know either,' said Clyde, wishing himself in Bruce's.

Lifelessly, he talked a little about Louis de Champêtre, squat and forbidding, nearing seventy and semi-retired, but still the undisputed head of the household and the family firm. No decision of consequence in either

44

domaine could be taken without his clearance. After breakfast, he spent the morning in the salon in pyjamas, a silk dressing gown and leather slippers, chain-smoking Gauloise cigarettes, reading *Le Figaro* and occasionally exchanging a word or two with his widowed sister, Madame de Vette, known as Didi, who sat with her back to the light, working at her tapestry frame. Around eleven, in time for coffee, his wife would join them, being eased into her red leather armchair by the maid who had washed her claw-like feet, helped her to dress and given her the medication prescribed for advanced diabetes and excess cholesterol.

'*Ça va, Tatou?*' Louis would call across to her, lowering his paper just long enough to catch her mumbled response.

A lifetime ago they had figured notoriously in Quebec society, carousing into the small hours, jumping into the sea hand-in-hand and fully clothed, being chased by police at a hundred miles an hour, their long scarves fluttering horizontally in the slipstream of their yellow and brown Bugatti. Today, soured by illness, their stiff and unwilling bodies were chauffeured to and from the homes of such friends as were still alive for cards or afternoon tea in the majestic black and silver V12 Lincoln sedan with whitewall tyres that was ever dear to Louis's heart and which he drove himself on Sundays.

Bruce said: 'But you won't live with the old couple again, will you, Clyde? You'll set up home on your own surely? You, Monty and Estelle.'

'She wouldn't hear of it. Estelle loves *Les Merles* and in time it will be hers. Estelle is set to become one of the richest people in the Province. Not only *Les Merles*, but the timber fortune and probably Didi's as well will fall into Estelle's lap.'

'I shall miss you when you go, CB – all three of you. I'm not a mixer, never have been, but the Beaumonts are the exception.'

45

'Estelle was telling me that your sister and her husband have taken Australian nationality and moved to Tasmania.'

'To Hobart. Ray's a motor mechanic and about to start his own business. He says mechanics are wanted all over Australia.'

Bruce reminded CB that he had lived with Joan and Ray Wallace between his parents' death and the Wallaces' emigration. By that time, he had switched from marine engineering to selling, following a correspondence course in salesmanship. He had moved to Hurworth because it was quieter than Bayswater and centrally placed on his territory.

'If I'd settled elsewhere, I wouldn't have met the Beaumonts,' he told Clyde, seeking to lift him out of his gloom, 'and I'd have been the poorer for it. I don't think I'd have continued at End Point without Estelle's encouragement and the useful riding tips she's given me.'

'You see only her good side.'

'She must be a social asset to a man in your position, Clyde. She knows how to behave, how to dress, how to entertain. I noticed her moving among your guests at your anniversary do, chatting with that Canadian consular official and the Master of the Hermitage Hunt and their wives. Estelle has this gift for making you feel you're the one person she'd hoped to meet.'

'I just wish we lived in an ordinary little house in a quiet turning, with nice neighbours and a garden to grow. She'd be a different woman without this family of hers and its love of money and power over other people.'

Bruce said: 'Estelle would be a different woman if she had a daughter.'

'She's told you?'

'When she was driving me home the other night. You'll have to get cracking, Clyde old boy.'

'She's knitting baby clothes. Pink. I asked if she had

46

any evidence. She said they're for the sale-of-work at St Mary's Church.'

'But you think they're for Aphrodite?'

'Who's he?'

'She. Goddess of fertility.'

'Oh.'

'Would you welcome an addition to the family, CB?'

'I'd welcome anything that got Estelle off my back.'

'I think you could use another pint.'

'I could use a gallon,' Clyde corrected, wryly.

Cameron looked back at him while being served at the bar. He envied him his fear of Estelle, of what she might do to him, but it was clear from Clyde's facial expression that, so far from sharing that sentiment, he was scared of going home to her.

'There's something on your mind, isn't there?' Bruce prompted, returning with the beer. He smiled. 'Is it business, CB?'

'I've tendered to the Liverpool Harbour Board for nearly a hundred thousand pounds' worth of timber, to be called off at quarterly intervals over a twelve-month period. I'll know at the end of this month whether my bid is acceptable.'

'How many sawmills are tendering?'

'Four. And we're the smallest. I made the mistake of telling my wife. She called Old Isoscelys at once. After talking it through with him, she told me I was to invite the Board's buyer to lunch at Orquinn's in Liverpool.'

'Not cheap.'

'He came and, yes, Estelle was as you've described her. By the time the check arrived, I had ceased to exist and he was ready to run away with her.'

'That doesn't mean you've landed the order.'

'Well, of course it doesn't, Bruce, but Estelle has convinced herself it's ninety percent ours and now it's for me to clinch it by telephoning this buyer every

47

Friday, by inviting him to inspect the mill and for drinks afterward at the Merton Hotel, by constantly asking if there's anything further we can do to secure the order. "Papa says to create a sense of obligation. Wear him down".'

'That's the way out, Clyde, not the way in. Unless he's on the make, you'll get the order if your price is right and you won't if it isn't. You'll get nowhere making a nuisance of yourself.'

'My sentiments exactly. When I said as much to Old Isoscelys, he broke into English and started shouting down the phone. I'm to get another interview with the buyer and leave him in no doubt that he is talking to the biggest timber people in North America. *"Don't kow-tow to this man. Are you there? Tell him les de Champêtre were in the lumber business before Liverpool had a harbour. Tell him! Tell him! And ask for the order".'*

'You won't get it.'

'I know.'

'Clyde: neither Estelle nor the old boy understands the tendering system. Perhaps it doesn't exist in Canada or it takes a different form. I can assure you that over here you don't buy or bully your way into someone's order book.'

'That's what I was about to say to the old tyrant when he slammed the phone down.'

'Lie to them, Clyde. Tell them you've done all the crazy things they've told you to do. On no account ask for the order. You'll kill it stone dead.'

The two men walked to their cars. Before parting, they shook hands and Cameron spoke of the forthcoming Sunday hack. But Clyde Beaumont wasn't listening.

'I was a fool to mention it to her. I could have left it out of the inquest and they'd have been none the wiser,' he muttered, with his faltering smile. 'Then, if I'd bagged the order, I could have said I was keeping it all as a surprise.'

'Think what a feather in your cap it'll be if you do bag it, Clyde!'

'Think what I'll get if I don't.'

3

Naked in the double bed at Hurworth and holding Estelle tightly in his arms, Bruce gently kissed her and asked if she would marry him if she were free.

She frowned and said, almost incredulously: 'You really mean this, don't you?' Then, when he made no answer: 'I'd be happy to think about it.'

It was the hour after love. The room was hot, flooded with sunshine, and Monty was at Bunty Hazelhurst's having his first piano lesson.

Bruce said: 'The Weasel. Don't like her. She's fake.'

'So? You're entitled to your prejudices just as I am to my opinions,' Estelle replied. 'It's a measure of Bunty's kindness that she's teaching my little cry-baby free of charge.'

'Is she qualified to teach?'

'Aren't you looking a gift horse in the mouth?'

'What do you know about her?'

'About Bunty? Only that life has been and still is a struggle.'

She had been born, Estelle went on, in a Shropshire village where the only industries were farming and coal mining. Her father and uncles had all been miners. Three eight-hour shifts kept the pit in operation round the clock from Monday to Saturday. Until she was ten, in 1950, there were no pit head baths and the terrace house that was home had neither running water nor sanitation. Using galvanised buckets, women carried water from a communal tap to their kitchen ranges to be heated for cooking and hip baths. Night soil was collected on Fridays from

49

outside lavatories by a man with a highsided horse-drawn cart. Bunty would never forget the stench, particularly obnoxious in the heat of summer, when bedroom windows had to be kept open, or the flies that were everywhere. She had been taught to play the piano by the parish priest and now, with much laughter between them, she was passing on her skill to Monty Beaumont.

'He was with us one afternoon at St Mary's Church, helping with the dusting and hoovering, when he started picking out a little tune on the piano. Bunty thinks he has talent, hence this afternoon. I left them sitting side by side and practising scales on her piano. If I know Monty, he'll soon lose interest.'

'Monty gets on well with people.'

'Yes, he does, even with Jack, Bunty's husband, who can be morose and touchy when not in his cups.'

'He was a child prodigy, I seem to recall her telling me.'

'Jack won the Elizabeth Grove Award in 1939 for Best Juvenile Actor and was unfortunately called up for war service quite soon thereafter. He's worth meeting, Bruce. Very English, like you. When he's the better for drink, he leafs through his scrapbooks of photos and reviews and shakes his head. But Bunty hides them when he's dry and irritable for fear he'll rip them to pieces or burn them.'

'I don't think I ever saw him in a film,' Cameron mused.

'Jack starred in four or maybe five movies and won his award for *Yourself And Fred*, which was his last.'

'I remember his stage name clearly enough. Sunny Picket.'

'He's rather proud of the fact that he came from nothing. Jack grew up speaking the fractured English you call cockney over here. He had difficulty with certain words, like water and butter, until the impresario, Clive

Valance, took a liking to him and sent him for acting and elocution lessons before giving him a new name and putting him on the stage.'

So far from paving the way to a distinguished career, Estelle explained, the Elizabeth Grove Award marked the end of Sunny Picket. As Corporal Hazelhurst, Jack returned to London from three years in a German prisoner of war camp to find that his father, assisted by more than one mistress, had squandered his fortune. His earnings as a child star had paid for a mansion in the fashionable London suburb of Norris Green, a Mulliner-styled Rolls-Royce and a modest staff of servants. His father, formerly a checker at West India Docks and for ten years his self-appointed manager, had filed for bankruptcy near the end of the war, partly the result of high living, partly of incompetence in investment management. When Jack traced him to Rowton House, Camden Town, he begged forgiveness on his knees and started weeping. 'Don't leave me to die, son. Don't leave an old man to die alone,' he called after him. But Jack did and at the time felt no remorse for having done so.

His disgust was compounded by his failure to revive Sunny Picket. Clive Valance found him a part in a cheap movie that was never released and he was in the cast of a West End production that didn't survive a provincial tour. By the end of the 1940s, approaching thirty years of age, he had to accept that Sunny Picket was finished.

'For years he drifted from job to job and place to place, often pursued by creditors,' Estelle said. She turned her head on the pillow to look at the alarm clock on Cameron's bedside table and told him she had time for a repeat performance. 'Dear little Montmorency thinks I'm at Quick's in Chester, having my car serviced.'

Bruce asked if Bunty and Jack intended getting

married. Surprised, Estelle countered with: 'Who told you they're not?'

'CB.'

'Don't repeat it. Bunty's never said why they haven't married and obviously I've never asked.'

'Why the secrecy?'

'Living in sin.'

Cameron dismissed the explanation with a contemptuous snort, leaving Estelle to continue with: 'Bunty gave him a home shortly after they met at a laying-on of hands at St Mary's. Jack was living in a men's hostel. She got him a job in the sorting office – she's a postwoman – but they fired him for smelling of liquor and now he just keeps house and paints a little.'

'Has Bunty never been married?'

'No. She says God was keeping her for Jack. She was sent to save him.'

'From work?'

'No one's going to give him a job at his age. When we first met him, he asked if we could find him something at the mill, but I had to say no. Alcohol and machinery are bad mixers. Let's make love while my Metro isn't being serviced. You're my hairy he-man and I'm impatient for results.'

'How's your less-than-hairy he-man? He seemed a little downcast last time we had a pot of beer together.'

'Clyde's been under a lot of pressure lately, but the end is in sight. It's my guess he'll be all smiles when you meet up on Friday.'

But Clyde didn't come to the Freemason's Arms. Bruce sat alone in the bar till half past eight, then drained his pint and made for the payphone, thinking that CB may have had trouble with his car or had met with an accident. He was about to insert a coin when a change of mind made him replace the receiver. If he drove to Gorman, he would see Estelle. Like Monty, she was a firesider who never went out in the evening except to confession on Saturday.

Clyde's Jensen was in its usual slot, parked neatly beside Estelle's red Metro. There was no lift in Oildrum Court, so Bruce walked up four flights of stairs to Flat 14 and for a minute or so stood listening before pressing the bellpush. He could hear Monty crying, his parents shouting, and Fiver, shut in somewhere, frantically barking and scratching on wood.

Bunty Hazelhurst finally opened the door. The boy was close to her side, as if held there, but he pulled himself free and ran, wailing, to the double bedroom.

'They're a bit busy just now, Brian,' Bunty confided, getting Cameron's name wrong and clearly intent on turning him away.

He wasn't having it.

Above the cacophony, he demanded: 'What's going on?', pushed the door wider and looked inside.

He could see into the Beaumonts' bedroom. Estelle had her husband flat against the wall, was holding his shirt-front with her left hand and shouting abuse into his terrified face, calling him Dumbell at the top of her voice and threatening to send him to work covered in bruises.

'Don't start on me again,' he bleated, on the verge of tears. 'How much more do you think I can take?'

Bunty said: 'He's just lost a big order. Better go now, Brian. It's not our place to interfere.'

'I don't need anyone to tell me what to do,' Bruce snapped. 'Least of all you.'

He looked again at the bedroom, sexually stimulated by what he saw and heard. Estelle, still berating her victim, was unaware of his presence and oblivious of Bunty and Monty. The boy, almost hysterical, was on his knees behind her, clinging with both hands to her skirt and pleading 'No, Mama, no!'

'I'll have to go to him,' Bunty said, urgently. She gave

53

a brief nod, said 'Another time, Brian, when it's blown over' and softly closed the door as Bruce stepped backwards onto the landing.

The row intensified as he went slowly downstairs. Two women and an elderly man stood listening outside their flats on the first floor and looking upwards at the Beaumonts' door.

Cameron paused. They heard Clyde shout 'Leave me alone. Leave me alone', then Estelle's 'Take your hands away from your face. Take them away!'

Now came the sounds of hard slapping and the bumping of Clyde's head against the hollow stud wall. His howling joined that of his son as the listeners heard Bunty call out 'Stop it, Estelle. Stop it! He's had enough', but to no avail. Estelle's rage was beyond her control.

Awestruck, one of the women said to Bruce: 'It's like a madhouse up there. She's been hitting him ever since he came home.'

'Should we tell the police?' the other woman asked.

'You won't get them out of their cars,' the man snorted, before turning away in disgust and stamping back into his flat. 'It takes a murder or a motoring offence to get *them* off their backsides.'

Chapter Four

Ravenous for her after witnessing her abuse of Clyde, Cameron made love with such passion that Estelle, amused as well as gratified, congratulated him on the vigour of his thrust but nevertheless turned down his invitation to return to Hurworth later that same week.

'You have your pots and pans and air rifles to consider,' she chided him, when they were getting dressed in his bedroom. 'They won't sell themselves.'

He took her, wearing only underwear and high heels, in his arms, in full erection again only minutes after coitus.

'You're eating me today,' she murmured, a little disturbed, a little puzzled. 'You need a replacement for Angela, Bruce, to satisfy your burgeoning appetite. Nice name, Angela. You must tell me more about her.'

'I don't want a replacement for anyone. I only want you, Estelle.'

'Hey, hey, hey!' she cautioned, placing her palms against his chest and looking with concern into his eyes. 'I have a husband. Remember?'

'He didn't show up at the Freemason's last Friday. What happened? I waited till my beer got cold. Wouldn't you let him go out? Did you make him scrub the floor because he'd been disobedient?' Cameron crooned with closed eyes, loving the words and the vision they raised of female domination and male submission. He kissed her, pressing her yet harder against his stiff manshaft. 'You told me there'd be something to smile about.'

Estelle tensed slightly and said: 'We're still waiting for news. CB didn't meet you at the Freemason's for the same reason that kept the Beaumonts from last Sunday's hack at End Point. Heavy colds. You won't see him this coming Friday either, because they're replacing a band saw at the mill and the work will be done over the weekend.'

'Which means I won't see you for supper on Friday night.'

'Righty. Unhug me now, if you please, so that I may finish dressing and collect dear little Monty from End Point before he starts thinking I've been sold into slavery. I suggest you take a cold shower.'

'Let me put your skirt on for you, Estelle.'

'You like this skirt, don't you? I might make you wear it one day.'

'Will you come here tomorrow, when Monty has his piano lesson?'

'I've already said no.'

'Please, Estelle!'

'We're meeting on Saturday, Bruce, in case you've forgotten.'

'We can't make love on the hunting field. Tomorrow! Just this once. Then I'll get back to my Tilley lamps and pea-shooters as if they're the greatest thing since baby's first smile.'

'I'm mystified. What's made you like a bull in heat all at once?'

'Say you'll come.'

'I can't, Bruce. Be told! When I dump Monty at End Point Riding Centre on Wednesday afternoons, the little innocent thinks I drive back to Oildrum Court, there to tell my beads till I return to collect him three hours later.

56

It works. But Bunty's lessons only last a half-hour. So that doesn't work. Once a week, my toad, must suffice.'

Dressed now, Estelle was repairing her make-up before Cameron's dressing table. He moved in behind her, still naked and upright, put his arms round her and kissed her ear.

'I'll just have to wait till Saturday then if you won't let me see you before,' he whispered.

'Get dressed!'

'Yes, mam. Yes, miss. Yes, my darling.'

'Leave me alone and put your clothes on. I'm running out of time.'

'What will I get if I disobey? A brisk spanking across your knee?'

Estelle met his eyes in the looking-glass and hers flared with distaste and vexation. 'When you talk in that sickly way, you make me think that even once a week is once too often,' she told Cameron, sharply. 'I only invited you to this Saturday Meet because the work at Britannia Mill will prevent Clyde from being with me. It's purely a one-off. Is that clear? Can you be at End Point and ready to mount at ten o'clock?'

'I can be on the moon or down a mineshaft if I know Estelle Beaumont will be there.'

'Stop being silly!' Estelle snapped. Then, frowning: 'You're on Countess. Monty will have our horses ready for us, so all you've got to do is be there.'

Her coolness continued into Saturday, much to Cameron's distress. After a curt 'Good morning', she pointedly avoided him until it came time to mount in the stable yard and accept a stirrup cup from Monty, who was circulating among the riders carrying a silver tray on which glittered flutes of champagne.

'I'm still a novice at hunting,' Estelle admitted, opening up a little. 'The chase, as they call it over here, is unknown in Canada.'

'What's the betting I fall off at the first fence?'

'Throw your heart over first. If Countess rears, tilt his head to one side. This will put him off balance and he'll have to come down. When his hooves touch the ground, send him forward on a circle. You'll have no trouble keeping out of the first flight because he's a plodder.'

'You've got Cromwell in a double bridle.'

'Because he's a puller.'

'You look lovely, Estelle, in your white stock and black bowler.'

She lowered her gaze as her features tightened.

'We'll be off shortly,' she said, checking Cromwell's girth. 'Here's the Huntsman joining us with his hounds. Those two riders with him in red coats and white breeches in need of cleaning are called whippers-in. They assist him in controlling the pack. The other man in red and white, wearing mahogany topped boots, is the Master of Foxhounds.'

'Major Shobbrook. We had a chat this morning. I told him I'm CB's stand-in, but not, I hope, his fall guy.'

'In that case, I've no need to present you. The Hunt Secretary is doing her rounds. Have you got your cap money for her?'

'Ten pounds.'

Estelle nodded her approval. All the followers – subscribers and visitors alike – were now gathered in the yard, chatting amicably atop horses whose eager anticipation of the chase was reflected in the restlessness of hounds.

'I want to hear about the time you came under police surveillance,' said an amused Estelle, as the Field rode out in rising trot. 'CB touched on it a few days ago, making it sound as coy as it was quaint.'

'Tell me first why you paid cap money. I thought you were a member of the Hermitage Hunt.'

'The Master wants me to be, but I can't make up my mind. Tell me: do you see hunting as cruel?'

'Not as cruel as angling. Not as cruel as rearing pheasants in release pens, where their wings are clipped and their beaks kept from closing by a steel bit inserted at the hinge of the jaw.'

'I'm forgetting. You're a shooting man.'

'Only clays. As for hunting, it is nowhere near as cruel as throwing live prawns and lobsters into scalding water, keeping a goldfish in a bowl or hens and calves in cages so small they can't turn round. Do you eat *pâté de foie gras*, Estelle?'

Looking uncomfortable, she said: 'I could hear that coming. You were about to tell me about Her Majesty's secret police.'

'I was about to tell you that I could never live in France because they support bull fighting and eat *foie gras* by the metric tonne. *Foie gras* is goose liver bloated by force-feeding the bird while it is held in a restraining device. It cannot move. It lives for only six weeks.'

'Papa would dismiss you as squeamish, but he would applaud your opposition to the Monarchy.'

'The Special Branch started taking an interest in me after I'd written two letters to the Queen and one to her son, calling him an aimless dullard.'

'Oh, goody! Do go on.'

'In all three letters I condemned their sybaritic way of life and urged them to curb their extravagance and reduce their dozen or more palatial residences to one town house and one country retreat. I suggested making these adjustments over a period of years, since it would be inhumane to suddenly release them and their kin into the cold air of reality. Remember there are numerous powdered flunkies and lickspital courtiers to be considered as well. The period of grace would permit these people to find alternative employment as the gradual conversion of palaces to communal use reduced the need for them.'

Estelle was smiling.

'Aren't you a rascal?' she hissed. 'But I like what I'm hearing. CB told me you signed your letters "Your bene-factor, Bruce Cameron", which is exactly what you are – you and the millions of other taxpayers in Britain.'

The pace sank to walk, then to halt, and Estelle explained that they were at covertside. 'Which means we must sit quietly while the Huntsman casts his hounds. See? He's sending them into that patch of woodland over yonder to flush Freddie Fox, sometimes known as Charley, should he be hiding there.'

Cameron looked beyond the assembled horses, statue-still for the most part, and their watchful riders in fawn breeches, black butcher boots, black or navy coats and black riding hats; beyond the Master, the Hunt Servants and the disappearing hounds; beyond all that to naked trees, black against a hard blue sky, to a hallowed church, hay-coloured in pale sunlight, to a manor house, and behind that the distant hills crowned with snow.

Hounds drew blank, so the Huntsman lifted them and rode on ahead to the next covert – a distance of no more than half a mile, but enough to allow the Field a long, thundering gallop and the challenge of three jumps.

'It's my inexperienced guess that we're not going to find,' Estelle said, when she and Cameron were reunited and sitting still at the check. 'You're out of breath. Calm yourself, sit deeper and leave the work to Countess.'

Bruce asked if finding meant flushing a fox and his companion nodded, uneasily yet pleasantly aware that he couldn't stop looking at her. They were far enough away from the rest of the Field to continue talking in low voices. She asked how he had known the police were watching him.

Cameron explained that at the time, which was shortly after his move from Bayswater to Hurworth, he used to jog on Saturday afternoons. One Saturday, a week or so after posting his third letter to Buckingham Palace, a young, dark-haired man, alone behind the wheel of a plain car, slowed beside him and stared across the road at him for a minute or so through his lowered window before driving on. Bruce was to see him again. He christened him Inspector Shy because he never approached Bruce or spoke to him.

'Moments after he'd driven off, a man photographed me as I jogged towards him, then quickly dodged out of sight into a side turning. By the time I reached the corner, he was sitting in the passenger seat of an unmarked car and being driven away at speed.'

'Goodness gracious! What convinced you they were police?' Estelle asked.

'Who else could they be? Hit men? Muggers? No. They were police all right and they proceeded to show their disapproval of my behaviour by appearing every Saturday afternoon for the next three months – not Inspector Shy, but each time a different man in a different car in civilian clothes. He would glide past me, stop about twenty yards ahead of me and pull away as I drew near.'

Estelle exclaimed: 'How marvellous! Were you scared?'

'Not after I'd talked it through with a solicitor, which I did soon after being photographed.'

'What did he say?'

'She.'

Bruce had shown her copies of his letters and asked her what action the police could take against him. 'None', she had answered. What he had written was legitimate criticism, astringent but in no way abusive or threatening. She felt he might possibly be charged with harassment, but concluded that it was unlikely because the Royal Family wouldn't want his comments aired in the media.

'And that was all?' Estelle prompted. 'Just these

strange men staring at you in their rearview mirrors before moving off?'

'That plus tapping my telephone.'

'You must tell me about that another time, when my husband is with me. I'm sure he'd like to hear it. The Huntsman's lifting his hounds again. That means another gallop in a minute or so. What was the reason for taking your photo do you think?'

'A print would be given to each of the Saturday drivers so that they could identify me. It was all a shameful squandering of police time and resources on the protection of one pampered family.'

'Not quite. They checked you out in case you were some kind of dangerous fanatic. I'll tell Papa your tale. He's a staunch republican who hopes to see Canada break away from the Commonwealth before he dies.'

Like most of the Hunt followers, Estelle and Bruce said goodnight around three in the afternoon. They made their way back to End Point, where their cars were parked, in trot and then in walk to cool and steady their horses. When smiling Monty asked how they had enjoyed their day, his mother replied that Major Shobbrook had apologised for failing to show them any sport.

'Sport, Mama calls it!' the boy declared, planting his fists on his hips. 'I ask you!'

Bruce wanted to know what Monty called it.

'Unpardonable barbarism,' he answered. 'Here! Give me your steeds, the pair of you. While you grab a hot cuppa, I'll serve them good clean hay and several buckets of cold water apiece.'

'Foxes kill lambs and poultry, Monty,' Bruce said. 'They've got to be culled somehow. The vixen kills to feed herself and her cubs. The dog fox kills for pleasure. There's an element of cruelty in hounding the fox, okay, but at least the kill is swift and clean, which

62

is more than can be said for shooting, gassing, trapping and poisoning.'

'We agree to disagree, Mr Cameron,' Monty concluded, jauntily.

Holding the reins slackly and just below the bit, he led Cromwell and Countess away to their stalls. His mother meanwhile said she was going into the social club for black coffee laced with rum.

'Tell me what you think of the sunset before you go,' Cameron said.

'The what? Oh yes. Rather grand.'

'This part of Cheshire is noted for them.'

'A good place for Bunty's husband to bring his stool and easel.'

The fierce, blazing red of the sinking sun turned the snow on the hills to pink and trimmed the scattered black clouds with gold. The background sky was a hazy blue shading to palest green at the horizon.

Standing close to her, Cameron tried to take Estelle's hand, but she turned away at the touch of his and walked ahead of him across the stable yard and into the club. She removed her bowler and shook-out her hair and sat down at a table while Cameron bought the coffee and brought it over.

'Thanks,' she murmured, without looking at him.

He lit his pipe, watching her over the flame, unsettled by her unrelenting coolness towards him.

'You haven't called me Bruce all day,' he chided her, in the lowest of low voices. 'You wouldn't hold my hand either.'

'You're fancy-free,' Estelle muttered, glancing round at the other people in the room. 'I'm not.'

'You wouldn't be safe if you were.'

Estelle sipped her coffee.

'What are your thoughts on fox hunting now that you've survived your first outing?' she asked, indifferently.

'I used to be hotly opposed to it, as I was to the Monarchy, wanting both abolished overnight; but I've cooled down a little since then. The majority of people who oppose hunting are lower class, like me, who, unlike my new self, vote Labour. They're mostly male and they harbour a deep, atavistic resentment of the man who looks down on them from a horse. In this country, he used to be the squire, the overseer, the gaffer, and they had to touch their caps to him. Today, he's the man who rides to hounds and they no longer have to defer to him. But the leering resentment is still there, and it's that, not sympathy for the fox, that is at the root of their opposition.'

Estelle's wandering gaze indicated that her thoughts were elsewhere.

Bruce asked if she would be coming to End Point for the hack next day.

'No. If CB doesn't have to return to the mill, I'll want him to rest. Monty'll be here.'

'I like Monty, but I'm not in love with him. When will I see you again, Estelle?'

'I'll call you.'

'Wednesday? At Hurworth?'

'I said I'll call you.'

'Yes, mam.'

'Here's Mrs Macdonald, looking as if she has something to say to me.'

'Another of your rubber cheques?'

Marilyn Macdonald was the proprietress of End Point Riding Centre, normally found in the retail shop. A smiling woman by nature, she now looked grave.

'Something's happened to Mr Beaumont,' she told Estelle, in a hushed voice. 'If you'll come with me, I've got a number for you to ring.'

Clyde was in intensive care. Estelle and Monty left at once for his bedside. Cameron telephoned the apartment that evening, but no one answered. Monty was not at End Point on Sunday afternoon. Cameron rang the apartment twice, in the morning and after the two o'clock hack, but still without getting a reply.

News of Clyde's death reached him on Monday morning, just as he was leaving home to begin a three-day stint on his territory followed by a day and a half in Birmingham at the annual sales conference of one of the three manufacturers he represented. The *Chester Chronicle*, handed to him by a newsboy through the window of his car, reported that Clyde had been driving to Gorman from Liverpool when his Jensen had left the road, burst through a hedge and slid twenty feet down a slope into trees.

No trace of drugs or alcohol had been found when he was admitted to hospital. A police statement indicated that he had, for no evident reason, lost control of his car at a sharp bend on a steeply falling gradient on a road he travelled twice a day five days a week. Accidental death would be the coroner's verdict, but it was and remained Cameron's belief that Clyde had chosen suicide as the only escape from his wife's bullying and those weekend conversations with her father that would have been an ordeal even if carried on in English.

Bruce was convinced that the slapping he had overheard was not the first she had given Clyde. There was cruelty as well as calculation in Estelle's nature. He believed her capable of deliberately driving her husband to suicide in the knowledge that her lover would marry her and in the increasingly desperate hope that he would father a girl while time was on her side.

But if such was her intention, she did nothing to

encourage Cameron during the week following Clyde's death. Contrary to Cameron's wishes, it was one of the busiest weeks in his experience, mainly because he had been neglecting his customers for the joy of sleeping with her. On three consecutive days, he made an early start, stayed late on his territory and telephoned Oildrum Court either before dinner at his hotel or after or both. If anyone answered, it was Bunty Hazelhurst.

'What's happening there?' he demanded, in a midweek exchange with this woman whose muted leave-everything-to-me voice annoyed him profoundly. 'Is Estelle all right?'

'She's distressed, Brian,' came the reply. 'She's in shock.'

'Well, put her on,' Bruce insisted, suspecting that The Weasel, for some reason, was blocking him. 'I want to speak to her.'

'She's asleep at the moment, Brian. I'll tell her you rang and she'll ring back. Okay?'

'I'm not at home.'

'Give me the number of your hotel and she'll get in touch.'

She didn't. When Bruce rang again, Bunty said Estelle was at the doctor's.

'Bring Monty to the phone.'

'He's with her, Brian.'

'Look! Tell her I'm anxious to help. I'll take Monty for a few days. He can come with me on my journey next week.'

'Monty is being well cared for, Brian.'

'Are you giving Estelle my messages?'

'Yes.'

'Then give her this one. I'll telephone tomorrow evening at eight. Got it? If that's not convenient, she has the number of this hotel. It's the one I've already given you.'

66

'And which I passed on.'

'Has a date been fixed for the funeral?'

'There's a memorial service tomorrow.'

'I'll be stuck in Birmingham all day and most of the next. I wish I could attend. Clyde was a friend.'

'Estelle isn't inviting anyone, Brian. Just her and Monty and a man from the sawmill has asked if he can come.'

'And you of course.'

'Well, I'll be playing the piano, yes.'

The more elusive she was, the more Estelle Beaumont dominated Cameron's thoughts. By day, he pictured her fingering soft brown hair away from one eye, tilting her head slightly and smiling at him. By night, when he lay sleepless in his hotel room, she was sitting in her armchair at Gorman, her thighs crossed, knitting and plucking at the hem of her navy skirt, staring pitilessly at her meek husband and saying: 'You're very quiet, aren't you? Have you made another mistake?' The vision made Cameron toss and turn, maddened by desire for her.

He had enjoyed a series of lovers in the course of his life, and Estelle, after realising that he was in love with her and judging it dangerous, had jollied him into talking about them. 'I met them at dances, preferring married women because they're easier to lay and I wasn't looking for a wife. Having to consider and consult someone would have slowed me down. What with my job, my interests and looking after myself these last few years, there was no time left for a companion.'

Estelle said, approvingly: 'Angela came closest to being one, from what you've told me about her.'

'I was lucky to have Angela. She was young – twenty-four, twenty-five perhaps – and married to a navigation officer with the Bell Line. She had a key to my bungalow. I'd come home to find her in my kitchen, preparing a delicious dinner for the two of us. "Reggie's away for a fortnight" she'd say, with her arms round my neck. And she'd be Mrs Bruce Cameron till the day before he docked at Liverpool.'

'A wife who isn't a wife. Every man's dream, I should think,' said Estelle, 'unless he wants to be a daddy.'

'She was my dream, that's for sure. A delightful brunette. She loved cooking and keeping house and having a man to tidy up after.'

'Did she love you?'

'No.'

'Did you love her?'

'No. It ended when she got pregnant.'

'By you?'

'By Reggie. Angela was always careful.'

Estelle said: 'You should marry, Bruce. You should have your own Angela.'

He answered: 'I've met her, but she's married.'

Women continued to admire his lean and muscular physique, his darkly handsome face, his relaxed and generous nature, his transparent integrity. 'No one man should have all that,' Angela had told her friend, never for a moment detecting the secret hidden within his masculinity, not even when his desire for the cane had prompted him to seek her reaction to an invented tale of a man of his acquaintance whose wife used to beat him at his request. She had shuddered and said: 'I've heard of men like that. Ugh! They make me feel sick.'

If Cameron had read Rousseau's *Confessions* instead of only his *Social Contract,* he might have been disabused of his conviction that he was alone in wanting to be maltreated as Estelle had maltreated Clyde. Like the Frenchman, he could trace his masochism and its attendant shame to a moment in his childhood. He had been about four, possibly five, when he had started trailing after his mother, begging her to whip him. What had lodged in his memory was her confusion,

68

her embarrassment, as she finally took gentle hold of his upper arm, gave it a little shake and brought her face down to his to tell him urgently that he must never say that again. Never. It was bad, bad. Guilt was implanted in that moment and still silenced his yearning to be bossed and beaten by an attractive and very feminine woman.

One such had been his sister, Joan, several years his senior, who had brought him up from the age of ten. Bruce had tried various stratagems to get her to chastise him, but she was by nature forgiving and incapable of hurting anyone. Corporal punishment by mistresses was neither illegal nor uncommon in his schooldays. Whilst he envied boys who received it, he was himself too orderly to deserve it and too shy of an audience to invite it. Later, he paid a prostitute to use his belt on him, but came away dissatisfied because he had had to tell her what to do and she had followed instructions mechanically, without passion and with a degree of perplexity. Bruce needed a woman with a temper, a woman who used words that excited him, a woman quick with her hands and born to dominate. He needed Estelle Beaumont.

He returned home on Friday evening with his imagination in a sexual ferment and shot through with the fear that she would return with Monty to Canada. 'You lovely bitch,' ran his thoughts. 'Where are you? Why are you hiding from me?' He had telephoned Oildrum Court at eight o'clock the previous night, as arranged with Bunty Hazelhurst, and got no answer. Estelle hadn't called his hotel and a message from her was not among those awaiting him on his answering machine. Was she laid low with grief? Not Estelle. Was she teasing him? No: that wasn't Estelle either. Then she was returning to Canada.

He dialled her number. If no one answered, he would

get back into his car without waiting to eat or drink and drive straight to Gorman.

To his fury, he got Bunty.

'Bring Estelle to the phone,' he commanded, without preamble. 'Don't tell me she isn't there, because I know she is.'

'She's a bit busy at the moment, Brian. Is there nothing I can do?'

'My name is not Brian,' Bruce shouted. 'Now put her on. I'm as much a family friend as you are and I intend to speak with her.'

'She's getting Monty ready for bed.'

'What! At seven o'clock? Now listen to me. You go to her and you tell her I'm coming to the flat if she doesn't come to the telephone. If she wants nothing further to do with me, I want it straight and I want it from her.'

A silence lasting no more than thirty seconds seemed to Cameron to go on forever.

Then: 'It's Estelle.'

Her voice was calm, heavenly, the bringer of intense relief but also of anxiety. Was she about to finish with him?

'Will you be at home tomorrow afternoon?' she asked.

'Yes,' he breathed. 'All afternoon.'

3

She didn't stay long. Because The Terrible Trio were performing outside, Cameron led the way into his office, where they were spared the clack and clatter of skate boards. He sat her down at his desk, seating himself on the straight chair that permanently stood beside it. She declined his offer of coffee or something stronger.

Faced with bereavement, he didn't know what to say.

'Words are all we have and they're not enough,' he

70

managed. 'It must be terrible for you, Estelle, especially when you wake in the night.'

'Always supposing I get to sleep in the first place,' she replied.

'And Monty?'

'He has dried his tears at last.'

'He loved Clyde.'

'He leaves the room whenever CB is mentioned. We need each other, Monty and I, as never before. We're only now beginning to accept that Clyde will never come home again.'

Estelle was pale, withdrawn, diminished, making Bruce ache to take her in his arms and kiss and comfort her.

She said: 'It's been easier for me because I've had the arrangements to make. Bunty has been solid gold, having Monty at her rooms when I've been with solicitors and accountants and of course Father Coglan.'

'I didn't know whether to send flowers,' Bruce admitted. 'Then, when I got home, I saw in the paper that you didn't want any.'

'Flowers only put money into florists' pockets,' Estelle answered. 'The dead can't smell flowers.'

Cameron was tempted to say that the dead can't hear a requiem Mass either; but instead he assumed aloud that Clyde was to be buried in Canada.

'Toronto. We leave as soon as the formalities are complete.'

'I'm lost in love for you, Estelle,' Bruce said, taking her hand in his. 'I'm sorry, by the way, about the last time you were here. I mauled you, didn't I? You should have slapped me.'

'It was nothing. I'd forgotten about it.'

'How lovely you look in black silk!'

'I'd better be going.'

'You know what I want to ask you, Estelle, but this isn't the time.'

'No.'

'How long will you be away?'

'Two weeks. A month maybe. There'll be lots to talk about at *Les Merles*.'

'But you will come back, won't you?'

Estelle stood up and replied: 'I'll have to. There's the apartment and the sawmill. I don't know yet what Papa wants doing about it.'

The couple were facing each other now, standing. Cameron took her other hand and looked into her sad eyes.

'Will you come out with me before you leave?' he asked. 'Just for a drive and a talk. You and Monty. We can have tea at the Devon Doorway and give Fiver a run on Thurstaston Hill.'

Estelle shook her head.

'I'll call you when we get back,' she promised. 'You've been a good friend to us.'

'I want to be more than that, Estelle,' Bruce said, opening his front door and standing aside. 'Safe journey, my darling. Take The Terrible Trio along will you? And leave them there.'

Estelle smiled and said goodbye before walking to her Metro, parked behind Cameron's Maxi on his short drive. After reversing into the road, she waved without looking at him. He watched till she was out of sight, then went back inside and closed the door.

4

Cameron scarcely crossed her mind during her time at *Les Merles,* but she thought more than once of the buyer from the Liverpool Harbour Board, who had attended the memorial service uninvited and afterwards had caught up with her and Monty as they walked between graves to the black limousine that would return them to Oildrum Court.

Raising his navy blue Homburg, he began: 'I don't expect you remember me, Mrs Beaumont. You and Mr Beaumont entertained me to lunch at Orquinn's earlier this year. Alan Reever.'

'Thank you for coming today,' Estelle said, accepting his card.

They shook hands and she introduced Monty. Mother and son, arm-in-arm and wearing black and white, were still subdued.

'My deepest sympathies to both of you,' Reever said, adding that he had seen the announcement of the requiem in the *Merseyside Express*. He lived on the Wirral.

'I liked Mr Beaumont,' he said, 'and felt great sympathy for him. I detected a worrier who took his work almost too seriously. He may have told you that he invited me to inspect the mill, while tenders were being considered.'

'My husband didn't tell me everything.'

'Afterwards we enjoyed a sandwich and a glass of beer together at the Merton Hotel, where my late wife and I had our wedding reception – a good many years ago, I have to say.'

Estelle smiled and nodded and thought how attractive the man looked in his city suit, white shirt, black tie and dark Crombie overcoat. He was taller and leaner than the sturdy and compact Bruce Cameron. Silver was evident in his black hair, kindness as well as melancholy in his handsome face. Estelle was getting to like Englishmen.

The trio stopped at the churchyard gate, where they were discovered by Bunty Hazelhurst, similarly on her way from the church to the limousine. Sensing that Estelle and Reever wanted a moment alone together, she promptly whisked Monty away 'so that Mama and the gentleman can talk quietly.' Later, to Estelle, she would

73

say with a smile: 'And who, pray, was that fine specimen I saw you getting pally with?'

Looking in admiration at Estelle, Reever said: 'I'm sorry we weren't able to give your company the order.'

'Our fault,' she answered. 'La règle du jeu. Obviously, our bid wasn't the lowest.'

'Oh, but it was, Mrs Beaumont, and I was ready to accept it until your father intervened.'

'Intervened?'

'He wrote to me from your headquarters in Quebec, telling me he was prepared to negotiate a price. I was duty-bound to include his letter with all the other tender documents when I made my presentation to the Board. As I feared, the vote went against you when it was seen that your sawmill was wholly owned by a Canadian company.'

Estelle murmured: 'You hadn't realised that earlier?'

'I knew you were Canadians, you and Clyde, but I was prepared to ask no further questions if you submitted the lowest quote, which in the event you did. After all, Britannia Mill has been established on Merseyside since the days of sailing ships. It employs Liverpool people. I liked you, both of you, your keenness and your sincerity. But the letter, or rather its provenance, got you black-balled.'

'I see,' said Estelle, quietly.

She nodded and, with lowered eyes, excused herself.

Neither Bunty nor Bruce Cameron voiced their suspicion that Clyde had committed suicide. As for Estelle, she firmly closed her mind to the possibility, never mentioning that, most unusually for him, Clyde had not been wearing his seat belt, and taking care not to visit the scene of the tragedy for fear of not finding skid marks on the road. To his parents in Toronto, and later at *Les Merles,* she variously blamed stress, anxiety, fatigue, for what she called the lapse of attention that had resulted in CB's death; but in secret, whilst not exonerating herself, she held her father responsible for it. His relentless pressure, coldly applied by Estelle, had reduced Clyde to a state of nervousness that opened the way to death by accident or by design. At Mass, on her knees between her parents and Monty, she asked his spirit to forgive her harshness, then resolutely wiped the past from her mind and looked ahead to the future.

'What's he like, this man who has written to you?' her mother asked, on the drive back to *Les Merles* and Sunday luncheon. 'How did he know where to find you?'

'He sent his letter care of Britannia Mill in Liverpool.'

'He wants to marry you, you say.'

'He's living on his own and driven nearly mad with loneliness. He lost his wife a year ago.'

'Can he give you the little girl you crave?'

'I didn't think to ask. He's fifty. Quite nice, only I suspect he's really looking for a mother.'

Within a single handwritten page, Alan Reever apologised for the timing of his proposal, explained that he had fallen in love with Estelle at Orquinn's and asked her to dine with him at the Grosvenor Hotel on her return to Gorman. He could offer Estelle and Monty a comfortable home and great and lasting devotion. Would she write to him? Would she telephone him?

'There's someone else besides,' Estelle told her mother, with neither pride nor satisfaction. 'Apparently, I'm irresistible.'

'English?'

'Yes.'

'Are you in love with him?'

'I haven't been in love, Tatou, since I was a young schoolmistress and he was deputy head.'

'The young man from Montreal. You brought him home to *Les Merles*.'

'I still think of him. I suppose he's happily married now with children. I hope so. He deserved happiness.'

'I'd like to see you married again, Estelle, but to a Canadian, preferably French, and this time to someone of your own class.'

'Not another *garçon de café,*' Estelle murmured, looking through her window at traffic waiting for the lights to change. 'Poor Clyde! He was the kindest of men, but I wasn't always kind to him.'

Unlike Louis de Champêtre, who had often sat staring at him in silence, Tatou had gradually softened towards CB, conversing as best she could given her neglected English and the speech impediment left behind by a stroke. Although it cost her an effort, she had talked to Clyde in her wobbly voice for a few minutes most days and Clyde had listened, smiling and nodding and understanding scarcely a word.

Estelle asked: 'Where would I meet this Canadian gent, Tatou, and how long would it take me to make him my husband? – always supposing he wanted a widow of thirty-five with a teenage son at foot. No. I'll have chosen my Englishman before Monty and I board our plane for England.'

The boy meanwhile was sitting in front of her, next to his irascible grandfather, who drove the Lincoln sedan with his head thrown back, his mouth open as if catching flies, and his old eyes screwed up and watering with the strain of staring directly and unswervingly ahead. Rather like an old dog who knows who is whom and what's what in a family, Monty regarded Old Isoscelys with undisguised amusement at his noisy and repeated clearing of the throat, his protracted blasts on the horn and vitriolic cursing of motorists who offended him. When not crowned by a garrison cap of black astrakhan, the old man's head, due to its shape and smallness, reminded Monty of a coconut, the scalp being covered with what looked like powdered rust, all that remained of a once thriving crop of ginger hair.

The boy had always brought out the best in him. When

he was small and running about, Louis had played hide-and-seek with him and tested his wits with such riddles as

> Patch upon patch without any stitches.
> If you can answer me that, I'll give
> you my breeches.
> What is it? A cabbage.
>   or
> Under the water and over the water
> and yet it never touches the water.
> What is it? An egg in a duck's belly.

Sometimes Louis had taken him to his office suite and sat him before a typewriter under the discreet watch of his secretary, Mrs Harvey, one of the few Champêtre employees unmoved by his sudden rages. Now that Monty was a big boy, albeit still in short pants, they no longer talked to each other through a pair of toy telephones, but instead played croquet on the spacious lawn, bordered by whispering aspens, at the rear of *Les Merles*. Louis taught him how to carve at table and how to tie a bow, although he was too young to dress for dinner as his elders did, Madame de Vette excepted.

Didi, as she was known, sat at one end of the rectangular table, her brother, Louis, three yards away at the other. She was eighty, with dishevelled hair resembling the thinnest fusewire, weeping eyes, and a trick of lifting her head slightly to peer through spectacles that were like silver discs when the light caught them. Heiress to a brewery fortune, she was grossly overweight, and slovenly in her food-stained black dress. Her aspect created a certain embarrassment within the family, especially when guests were present, and occasionally gave rise to acrimonious exchanges with Tatou, her sister-in-law, who, like Estelle, was meticulously clean in habits and attire, invariably clad in a slim, full-length dress with a lace collar, her neatly dressed hair reminiscent of a head of broccoli, only snow-white instead of greenish-brown. Diabetic feet confined her mostly to her red leather armchair, always with two walking sticks leaning against it, unless Monty had placed one over the other and was entertaining her with a sword dance.

Tatou's sight was still sharp enough to permit the enjoyment of the great French novelists, Proust and Colette excluded, but the stroke that had slurred her speech had also disturbed her equilibrium, causing her upper body, when seated, to slowly tilt in what Monty described as a slight list to starboard. Since the old lady was helpless to correct it herself, he would take her by the shoulders and gently restore her to the upright position. Once there, she would read *Le Figaro* after Old Isoscelys had finished with it or watch the television that was left on all day, usually with the sound turned low. Inhibited by her infirmities, she seldom conversed, preferring to sit in po-faced silence, her prim little mouth firmly closed above a cutback chin, her hands lightly clasped in her lap, the veins as prominent now as a tree's exposed roots.

Such conversation as there was in the salon at *Les Merles* was shared unequally between her sister-in-law, sitting at her tapestry frame in the bay window, and her husband, seated beside a smoker's stand with a lid that could be made to rotate by pressing a black knob in its centre. As sporadic as it was perfunctory, the exchange was dominated by Louis, whose creeping deafness made him put his hand behind his ear and shout '*Hein*?' when unable to catch what Didi was saying. In contrast to her quiet voice, his loud and often irritable responses could be heard all over the house.

For the duration of their stay, his daughter and grandson softened the old patriarch, reducing his awareness of the gout that tormented him and the restraints imposed by high blood pressure. Like Tatou and Didi, like the smiling servants who had welcomed them home, he wanted calm Estelle and spirited Monty to stay at *Les Merles* for good.

'Find a buyer for Britannia Mill, Estelle, then you and Scamp hop aboard the next flight back to civilisation,' he said, at dinner one evening. 'Forget this bounder who wants to marry you. He's only after your money.'

'Scamp!' Didi exclaimed, quietly and with relish. 'I like it.'

She smiled fondly upon the delicate boy, whose peerless skin, blue eyes and ash blond hair had made her exclaim '*un bébé anglais!*' when Estelle had brought him home from the maternity hospital.

'Two bounders, not one, are after Estelle's money,' Tatou yodelled. 'Our daughter, my clown, is as much in demand in England as Penelope was in Sicily.'

'It's news to me that Mama has a brace of admirers,' Monty chirped, bouncing in his seat. 'Till just this moment, Scamp knew of only one.'

'Scamp is not too old to be sent to bed,' Estelle warned him. 'I don't want to hear another word from you on that subject, so eat your dinner and don't speak again until you are spoken to. I think you were about to say something, Didi.'

'Only that I think it's right that you should marry again, Estelle, if only because Monty is coming to the age where he needs a father.'

'Must he be English though?' Louis questioned, watching the parlourmaid serve dessert. He turned to Monty with: 'And what about you, young man? Would you be happy living permanently on foreign soil?'

'It may not be permanent,' Estelle murmured.

'I don't care where I live so long as Mama's there,' replied Monty.

There were many features of life at *Les Merles* that

appealed to mother and son alike, from total immersion in French to the faded elegance of their surroundings. Monty loved the two old ladies. He chatted with them, saw they were comfortable, and stirred memories of bygone days with records as thick as dinner plates, which he dusted and played on the Kolster cabinet gramophone that had stood in silence for years. He explored his grandmother's library of French literature and English classics in translation or played on the carpet with the exquisite Burmese kittens, Toupineau and Toupinette.

After one morning on the slopes, Estelle decided she had lost her enthusiasm for skiing. There was more pleasure, she found, in talking with Tatou over her knitting and with the rest of the family at dinner. This was a candle-lit ritual over which Old Isoscelys presided in black bow, black braided trousers, patent leather shoes, silk socks and a white tuxedo. The food at the polished rosewood table was of the finest and most varied, faultlessly cooked and served, preceded by dry sherry and accompanied by Château Lafite and an excellent white Bordeaux, often Château d'Yquem. Louis dismissed cocktails and a well-known brand of Scotch whisky as fit only for Americans.

Sometimes there were guests – never more than two, often only a singleton, the priest perhaps or the family doctor – and they would stay for bridge. Old Isoscelys, having studied his hand, would declare the bidding open with a loud '*Parole!*' Monty would cleave to his mother, watching the play but with no desire to take part, leaving her side only to restore his tilting grandmother to the perpendicular. The old lady shared with the others a deep and abiding love of contract. While Estelle was there to make a fourth, they played every evening.

But the time came for the Beaumonts to leave for England, and for Estelle, through a commercial estate agent, to find a buyer for Britannia Mill. When next

Bunty Hazelhurst telephoned *Les Merles,* she asked her to arrange for a taxi to meet their return flight.

'Is it raining in England?' Tatou asked, when her daughter returned to the salon.

She posed the same question every Wednesday after Bunty had called from Oildrum Court, where she had checked that all was in order and opened such letters as Estelle wanted read to her. Monty, as ever, was at his mother's elbow, awaiting his turn to speak with Bunting, as he called her, and to hear Fiver bark in response to the calling of his name.

'Our dog is staying with the Hazelhursts while we're away,' Estelle explained, adding that the couple were loyal friends, always ready to help when help was needed.

'It's my guess you'll settle in England, Estelle, and I could wish it otherwise,' Tatou warbled. 'England's gain will be Canada's loss.'

'You know the reason and it's the only reason.'

'Have you made your choice between the two scoundrels who are seeking your fortune?'

'Yes, Mother, I have.'

Chapter Five

The marriage was witnessed in the Chester Register Office by Bunty and Jack Hazelhurst, who later took Monty for a week-long stay at the Retreat House in the grounds of Stanmore Abbey while Estelle and her new husband drove north for a week's trail riding in the Scottish Borders.

'I hope she's made the right choice,' Bunty said, her tone implying that she hadn't. 'What do you think, Jack?'

'Can't say, because I never saw Alan Reever.'

'I thought him old-fashioned myself and a bit like an undertaker. Estelle showed me the letters he sent her when she was in Quebec. He'd lost his heart to her all right. She let him take her to lunch at the Grosvenor Hotel and that's when she decided on this Brian.'

'Bruce. I like him. We had some amusing sessions at the Racquets Club in the run-up to the wedding. Together, we founded the First Church of Christ Humanist to compete with the established church of Christ Scapegoat.'

'Could we talk about something different, beloved? Cameron won Estelle because she didn't want a man she could push around. She hasn't said nothing to me, but I think her conscience is troubling her.'

By the end of the luncheon, Estelle had revised her first impression of Alan Reever, moving nearer to Bunty's assessment of him. Misty-eyed devotion and full lips as red and fleshy as an overripe strawberry had warned her that she was facing a man whose yielding nature might tempt her to drive and dominate him.

'What did Estelle say when you telephoned her last night?' Jack asked.

'Only that they'd arrived safely and the weather in Jedburgh was brilliant.'

'Like it is here. What did you say the Guest Mistress's name is, Cock?'

'Cock! Sister Francesca. She has charge of the Retreat House. Attractive, isn't she, in her black and white?'

'Every woman is attractive in black and white. The combination does something to a man.'

'Was it Leonardo da Vinci or Michelangelo who carved the magnificent *Pietà*?'

'Michelangelo Buonarroti. Interesting, don't you think, that we call some artists by their first names but not many? We call Scott Fitzgerald Scott even in scholarly assessments of him, but no one refers to James as Henry or to Hardy as Thomas. It's as though we knew Scott and liked him and felt a little responsible for him. He did our living for us, not to mention our drinking.'

'Quite frankly, I'm more interested in Michelangelo,' Bunty responded. 'And what I wanted to say, beloved, before you went off at a tangent, is that Michelangelo claimed that chaste women age more slowly than the unchaste and that their skin is whiter. And it is. Look at the sisters while we are here at Stanmore and see how their skin is like candlewax. Incidentally, dearest Jack, I might remind you, before you take another of your swipes at my religion, that it is thanks to papal patronage that Michelangelo has left us the decorated ceiling of the Sistine Chapel and his painting called *The Last*

Judgement. Shall we walk a little? I want you to see the grounds while the sun is on them.'

'Nuns scared me when I was a nipper, all in black except for a white wimple stiff with starch,' Jack recalled, taking Bunty's hand. 'They went about the East End on foot, always in twos like the coppers did, never smiling, collecting Peter's Pence from door to door. They had a rosary hanging from the waist and wore polished black leather shoes that squeaked and they didn't like children. Mind you, we were urchins most of us, the boys wearing boots, pullovers and short pants like Monty's, sometimes with a patched seat or no seat at all. We lived in tenements. The thin, tart smell of stale underwear and unwashed bodies hit you the moment you stepped inside.'

'I remember that smell, a sour smell, as I remember the stench of night soil. People today, with their bathrooms and washing machines and televison sets, can't imagine what it was like.'

Always with time on his hands now that he was in his sixties, Jack sometimes talked of life before the Welfare State with their landlord, Bill Bushell, who shared many of the Hazelhursts' recollections of penury and hardship. Once, when unemployed in the 1930s, he had walked from London to Brighton after hearing there was work in one of the hotels. Laughing, he would say to Jack 'Them days are gawn and parst, mate.'

'He was a boy in Hackney when I was living in Dockside, before Clive Valance turned me into Sunny Picket and transformed my life,' Jack told Bunty. 'Bill's father was a rag-and-bone man, trundling a handcart round the slums, buying and selling old clothes and sharpening kitchen knives.'

The Bushells had left 'dear ole London' early in the 1950s, drawn to 'the Norf' by well-paid opportunities for upholsterers in the Merseyside car plants. They were

84

small, cheerful, benign people. Mrs Bushell was plump and baby-faced, a local councillor and active in the Townswomen's Guild. She had met Bill shortly after the Second World War, when both were employed in a mental hospital, she as a vegetable cook, he charged with fitting-out and maintaining padded cells. Smiling and bespectacled, he stood with his knees slighlty bent and his shoulders hunched, giving Jack the impression that he had been taken short and was trying not to notice it.

Retired now, the couple owned the house in Meadows, opposite St Mary's Church, in which Jack and Bunty rented a double bedroom and the front sitting room. High ceilings and naked linoleum floors with only a rug here and there made their rooms clattery and so expensive to heat that in winter they huddled round their puny coal fire wearing mittens and outdoor clothes. The furniture was cheap and bruised and included, in the sitting room, an upright piano made long ago in Germany by Rud, Ibach Sohn, out of tune and with two dumb keys, but good enough, in Bunty's words, for young Monty to bang about on.

'Having said that, he now wants to learn properly,' she told Jack. 'I said all right, but he'll have to practise at home between lessons, so Estelle's going to buy him a piano.'

'Second-hand.'

'You know Estelle.'

'She'll make him use it too,' Jack said. 'She'll want a return on her money.'

'Use time: never kill it. That's what Estelle drums into him. She won't let him watch television, you know, except as a reward for doing something constructive. Poor Monty! But he's happy.'

He and the Hazelhursts had arrived at Stanmore the previous evening, located their bedrooms in the Retreat House and then gone down to the dining room, where a cold, self-service supper was laid out. After a night's sleep, they had helped themselves to breakfast in the guest-kitchen, returning at one o'clock to the dining room for a two-course luncheon in company with a dozen or more talkative retreatants seated at refectory tables. With the dessert, Jack and Monty got to their feet to be introduced to Sister Francesca.

'Call me Frankie,' she said, to their surprise. 'If there's anything you want while you're in the House, Bunty will point out my lair. Bunty of course is one of our regular customers, if Our Lord will forgive me for making Stanmore sound like Sainsbury's.'

Smiling, she glanced at the large crucifix that looked down upon them from the wall above the serving hatch. Then she looked at Jack and approved of what she saw.

When he asked if he might set up his easel in the grounds, she felt no surprise at this evidence of his artistic bent. He looked the part in his brown velvet corduroy jacket, fawn moleskin trousers, slip-on brown leather shoes and a check shirt with a Paisley cravat filling the open neck. His presence was self-assured and commanding, his voice stage-trained and kept steady and mellifluous by regular gargling with vinegar. Before the end of the week, she would smile at his monocle, his buttonhole (a carnation, sometimes a gardenia) and his rattan cigarette holder.

He would not have amused Bunty's mother, long since laid to rest in the Shropshire mining village called Streets, where Bunty had been born in 1940. Her father, a miner, had died in a pit disaster, leaving her mother to survive on a company pension augmented by what was then called National Assistance. By this time, Bunty was working as a maid at the local presbytery, returning home to cook and clean and fill buckets at the communal tap until piped water and sanitation arrived in the 1960s. Villagers remembered her as the pale and harassed slave of her old mother, Bridie Flanagan, confined by arthritis to a wheelchair, her nature twisted and embittered by nagging pain that triumphed over the strongest painkillers. 'I wish we was 'ome,' she would bleat, when being pushed along by her perspiring daughter. 'So do I, Mother,' Bunty would answer, weary in body and spirit alike; but once returned to her place beside the kitchen range, she would fall to complaining of being 'stuck in 'ere till kingdom come' and perhaps taunt Bunty about not having a young man to take her out.

'What chance have I got of meeting boys?' Bunty would mutter, aware that it was not so much opportunity she lacked as feminine appeal. A dance was held on Saturday nights at the Parish Hall, but she declined another girl's invitation to attend in the belief that no one would ask her to get up. She was regarded as a funny little woman, tripping along with short, quick strides in shoes half a size too big for her, bare-legged even in winter and always in the same dowdy clothes.

Then came Leon, newly arrived in Streets with his parents and working in the wages office at the pit where Bunty's father had met his end and to which she went every Friday to collect her mother's pension. They started going for walks together, and in time she brought him home.

Awed by him at first, almost to the point of dusting the seat before he sat down, Bridie gradually decided he was nobody and a snob. The doctor apart, he was the first man in clean clothes ever to enter her two-up-and-two-down. 'Does his mother dress him?' she demanded of Bunty, referring to his Weaver to Wearer suit with all three buttons fastened and the macintosh folded with barrack-room neatness and carried over the forearm when not worn. 'Oh, and with his gloves!' the old crow would sneer, her resentment gathering force. 'His leather gloves, fleecy-lined an' all'; and, with her nose in the air

87

and her lips pushed forward, she would make as if drawing gloves over her hands and kneading them snugly into the spaces between her fingers. 'Him with his oiled hair and his quiff and his fancy ways. He's not from our stable, Bunty.'

'Leon is a gentleman, Mother.'

'Lord Muck. Lord Muck. That's who he is. Lord Muck.'

'You'd like to see me married to Jimmy Devine, I suppose? A scruffy little railway porter, twice my age, with wandering hands and foul breath.'

'He's working class and you can't beat the working class,' Bridie declared. 'They've got the guts. They've got the guts.'

Jack Hazelhurst's smile broadened as Bunty paused to admire the view.

'You've never mentioned Leon till now, you dark little horse,' he chided her. 'You didn't marry him, but I think you wanted to.'

'He didn't marry me.'

'You didn't marry the railway porter either.'

'Death first.'

'Your mother would have approved of me before Clive Valance turned a sow's ear into a silk purse,' Jack said. 'You're looking at a fraud, a fake, the invention of acting teachers and voice coaches, a window display with an empty shop behind it.'

'You're my chap,' Bunty answered. 'That's all that matters to me.'

Their walk ended in the rose garden, where they sat down in wicker tub chairs, facing the sun and with their backs to the Retreat House. Monty had gone to the village to buy a picture postcard to send to Mama and Ibzy (his name for his stepfather) and a packet of cigarettes for Jack, who was smoking between thirty and forty a day.

'I do wish you'd stop it, beloved, before it stops you,' Bunty said, and went on to remind him of how she had at last conquered the habit, urging him to follow the same procedure. It had worked, she said, for two of her colleagues in the sorting office, as well as for the sexton at St Mary's Church.

'Don't make the mistake, Jack, of throwing your cigarettes and matches into the fire on New Year's Eve and saying "That's it! I'll never smoke again", because, quite frankly, from that moment onwards you'll be haunted by the longing for a smoke. Instead, start a little later each day and keep your cigarettes and matches within reach so that you'll feel stronger than them. Within a week, you'll be lighting your first cigarette at eleven in the morning instead of earlier; then delay the start till after lunch and go on delaying it until eventually you reach nine o'clock at night, by which time you'll say to yourself "I might as well wait till tomorrow now". Within a matter of weeks, you'll be rid of the habit. But never say "I'm finished". If the longing for a fag gets unbearable, have yourself a fag. It's not the end of the world. But after a couple of puffs, when you go dizzy and your heart starts bumping, you'll think "I'm sorry I did that" and you'll stub it out and your will to stop will be stronger for the lapse. Will you at least give it a try?'

Jack found Bunty's hand in the gap between their chairs and clasped it.

'When you're an old geezer like me, you'll ask yourself two questions every day,' he predicted. 'Number one: when will death come? Number two: what form will it take? I don't want to die in public because I consider it bad manners, or, as Clive Valance used to say, *damned* bad manners. I want at least three days' notice so as to cancel the milk and cut my credit cards in half.'

'You haven't got any credit cards,' Bunty laughed, 'and it's me who orders the milk.'

'The grandees of long ago were buried with pots and pans, gold and silver and myrrh for use in the next world. All I want in my coffin is my bottle opener. What I'm saying, Bunty, is that at sixty-plus you become very conscious of time running out. You mean well when you lecture me.'

'I never lecture you, Jack, ever.'

'You're only old once, so make the best of it: that's my motto. I'm sitting in the departure lounge, waiting for my flight to be called. Leave me to enjoy my cigarettes and whisky.'

'I'm only thinking of your health, Jack,' Bunty said. 'I don't want to lose you.'

But she was thinking too of their financial situation. Jack's unemployment benefit was absorbed by his daily indulgences at the Racquets Club, whilst Bunty's wages from the Royal Mail covered their domestic expenses. There was nothing left over for holidays, clothes or emergencies, which was why Bunty was grateful to Estelle for financing their week's stay at Stanmore Abbey. Extra money would come from the same source for Monty's weekly piano lessons, each lasting an hour and scheduled to begin as soon as the Camerons were established at Hurworth.

'I'm going to pray for Estelle while we're here. I'm going to ask God to send her a little girl,' Bunty said. 'She's already got a name for her.'

'As well as baby clothes.'

'Dawnia. Dawnia Cameron. Nice, isn't it, beloved? Will you promise me something, Jack? Will you come with me and Monty to compline after supper? They pronounce it complin, by the way. It's the least the three of us can do to show Sister Frankie we're not treating the Retreat House as a hotel. I'll go to Mass every morning, and Estelle wants Monty to go too, but you'll likely want to paint.'

'I'll come to compline if you'll come with me to the Bluebell after Monty's gone to his room. It's only five minutes down the road.'

'I know where it is. Opposite the post office. Well, nearly.'

'I noticed it yesterday from the taxi.'

'Somehow I thought you would.'

'Have they got television here, Cock?'

'I'll show you as we go in to supper.'

'I want to watch the Ashes. Monty might want to as well.'

'What are these famous Ashes? Who was it, by the way, who called cricketers flanelled fools?'

'Same man who called footballers muddied oafs. Kipling. The Ashes are the charred remains, hand rubbed to a fine powder, of the last pair of drawers known to have been worn by W.G.Grace.'

'Quite frankly, I consider football a ridiculous game,' Bunty said. 'Grown men playing ball and shouting to each other!'

'Kissing and spitting in one another's faces.'

'It's as silly as its name. Football! Estelle has give me a hundred pounds to cover our taxis, plus treats for Monty. I'll take him into town on the bus tomorrow. He wants to buy a present for Mama.'

'See that splendid cedar of Lebanon over there? The tree with the slatted wooden seat built round it?'

'I've been known to sit there when it's sunny,' Bunty said.

'Well, I'm going to ask Frankie if I can set up my easel there and start sketching them thar hills.'

In the course of the week, when she sat with him for a few minutes each day, Jack told Frankie that his creativity was stirred at irregular intervals and at all sorts of odd moments. He could be cleaning Bunty's motor scooter or playing cards at the Racquets Club when the germ of an idea would make him reach for pencil and paper. Once indoors, he would elaborate the idea on his sketch pad, then lay it aside for a day or perhaps as long as a week before developing it into a picture. He painted at night, after Bunty and the Bushells had gone to bed, working on into the small hours and ending up after three or four nights with a passable landscape or still life.

'I can hear Dublin in your voice, Sister,' he told her one morning. He spoke approvingly, conscious of Dublin's glorious contribution to the creative arts. 'So tell me what prompted you to come here as an enclosed nun of the Benedictine Order.'

'Our Lord prompted me.'

Francesca was not her given or 'home' name: that was Teresa; and Dublin, she confirmed, was her birthplace. A convent education and the influence of two nun aunts had prepared her, subconsciously at first, for the religious life.

'When I was twenty and living at home, I heard for the first time the Gospel passage "Leave everything and follow me" and recognised it as speaking to me. So I wrote to contemplative communities in England and America, where my mother has relatives, asking if I might come and stay in the enclosure. I had many responses, much the most positive from Abbess Amanda of this abbey.'

Frankie had spent ten days at Stanmore, had then applied to enter, and was accepted as a postulant.

'That's not the same thing as a novice,' she told Jack. 'Some people think it is. An entrant is a postulant for six months before becoming a novice. The novitiate lasts for two years and the novice wears a white veil. Her temporary vows end finally with consecration to a life of piety and celibacy.'

'Bunty sometimes wishes she had been a nun.'

'I know. When she stays here, she attends all five

92

divine offices every day. Yesterday was an exception because she took Monty into town.'

An hour or so at the Bluebell after the boy had gone to bed became habitual for the duration of the retreat. The heatwave that developed persuaded Jack to dress up in striped blazer and white flannels, which, combined with brown-and-white spectator shoes and a Panama with the brim pulled down all round, caused a mild sensation among the locals. The thespian in him blossomed in the warmth of admiring attention, inducing a sense of well-being that he sought to deepen and prolong by graduating from beer to whisky and drinking enough of it to make him disregard Bunty's sensitivity concerning religious matters.

'I could see you as an apostolic nun, going out into the community to help and sustain people, but not as an enclosed one, like Sister Frankie,' he told her. 'I'll bet a pound to a penny she views her life here, in what she calls this power house of prayer, as one of self-denial, when it's obviously the precise opposite. She and her chums have withrawn from society to look after themselves and each other and to pray for the best seats in the next world. Nuns and monks are drop-outs, Bunty. So was Jesus. I can't accept his divinity, which devalues him, but I respect him as a fearless preacher with neither time nor patience for the dogma and ritual associated with church and clergy. His message was and remains as simple as it is inconvenient: SIN NO MORE!'

'The bar is filling up,' Bunty remarked, looking round the room.

But her chap was not to be discouraged.

'It was Paul, sometimes known as Saul,' he went on, 'who made the dead Jesus, an Asian Jew, the figurehead of the Faith we know as Christianity, but which ought to be called Pauline Christianity, because it's as far away from the teachings of Jesus of Nazareth as Mars is from

Jupiter. Yours is the religion of weaklings and hypocrites, confessing the week's sins on Saturday and having them absolved next morning by the symbolic eating and drinking of a man's flesh and blood. The doctrine of redemption through the atonement is as cowardly as it is convenient.'

Bunty said: 'Don't look now, beloved, but I think Sunny Picket has been recognised. The foursome sitting in the bay . . .'

'Drink up, Cock,' Jack muttered. 'We're leaving.'

2

The Camerons did most of their talking in bed – before, between or after love-making. Over an average weekend, they were together as many as five times, including Saturday afternoons, when Monty was working at End Point; so that it was with concealed relief that Bruce, as weak as Samson after a haircut, kissed his wife goodbye and got into his car on Monday morning. He needed the rest of the week to get his breath back.

He left behind a mother at odds with herself over her son, wanting him to become a man yet at the same time loath to lose the little cry-baby whom she could sit on her knee and kiss and cuddle and soothe with pet names and endearments following mishap or corporal punishment.

'Monty needs you, Ibzy,' she made herself say. 'Will you take him with you once in a while on your week's journey? I'll pay his hotel expenses.'

'I've already suggested it, Estelle, more than once, but he just smiles and changes the subject. Swimming with me before Sunday breakfast and our drive to the car wash is the best I've been able to manage.'

'I've got him using your body-building contraptions in the conservatory,' Estelle said, omitting to mention

94

that Monty called it the torture chamber and wanted to see it emptied and filled with flowers, which he pronounced flars. 'I send him in there while I'm preparing lunch.'

But the boy was back at his mother's side within minutes, standing close to her with his arm round her waist and saying: 'What are you doing?'. More at home in the kitchen than elsewhere in the bungalow, he was already capable of cooking and tastefully serving a three-course dinner. His bread and cakes approached professional excellence, prompting Bunty Hazelhurst's comment that boys make light pastry thanks to their strong fingers.

Estelle was preparing him for GCSE examinations, to be taken as an external candidate, in English, French, history and mathematics. From Monday to Friday, they would work together from nine till twelve in the room known as the office, the room in which Bruce had done his telephoning and clerical work on Saturday mornings ever since moving to Hurworth.

'Is Monty a good pupil?' he asked, while naked in bed with his wife. 'Diligent? Obedient?'

'Brighter than most, I'd say, but inclined to daydream. If he works well, I take him shopping in the afternoon, and sometimes, as a special treat, we have tea and cookies at the Devon Doorway.'

'And if he doesn't? Smack, smack, smack?'

'He goes over my knee and spends the afternoon in his room with the shades closed.'

The couple kissed, Cameron taking his time, relishing Estelle's words as his lips squirmed over hers.

'What do you use on the poor mite?' he said in her ear. 'A strap?'

'My ruler. But never mind that. Let's be nice to each other again before I have to fetch the little darling from End Point.'

Yearning to change places with Monty but too guilt-ridden to admit it, Bruce, in proud erection, pumped hard, his performance invigorated by the image of Monty lying face down across Estelle's accommodating thighs while she called him a naughty little boy and made him writhe under a brisk spanking. He had married in the belief that she was going to treat him as she had treated Clyde, only to find that her motivating zeal had moved from her late husband to her son during the months that separated CB's death from her second marriage. When Bruce had for the first time told her that he wasn't going to Mass with her and Monty, he had done so in the hope that she would answer coldly 'Oh yes you are!'; and when he announced that he was off to his Lodge, he waited to hear 'No you're not'; but in place of those magic words of command and prohibition, there came only a casual 'Righty', as if to say 'What are you telling me for?'

Eventually, Cameron had to accept that he was wanted solely for breeding. Love-making with Estelle was strictly functional. She wanted Dawnia. Any form of dalliance, of lovers' amusements such as pillow fights or wearing each other's clothes, was beside the point. The closest Bruce could get to being dominated by his wife was to become her pupil, which he did after asking her to do for him what she had done for CB.

'And what does that mean?' she asked, smiling. 'If it means putting you in charge of Britannia Mill, you're a little too late, Ibzy, because I've found a buyer at long last. I can't tell you how glad I am. I hated driving to the Odious City every week for talks with the Ancient Mariner, as CB used to call his deputy, plus sundry accountants and attorneys. God willing, I'll be officially rid of it at month's end. I could have sold it ages ago, but Papa wouldn't budge an inch over the price.'

Cameron said: 'I want to be a sales manager with a

decent company, Estelle, and I want you to be my inspiration, as you were Clyde's.'

'Why not a sales director, my toad? Where's your ambition?'

'It needs prodding. I thought I'd start by learning French and maybe taking a correspondence course in marketing.'

'If you want to learn French, Bruce, step into the office and we'll start right away. I love teaching.'

'I want you to work me hard, Estelle. Teach me to read, write, speak and understand the language. Don't let me off lightly because I'm your loving husband. Make me learn it thoroughly and properly.'

'*Ça va de soi, mon enfant.* I don't recognise any other way. You get it right or you do it over again.'

That closing imperative defined a teacher-pupil relationship that Cameron found sexually stimulating. It ran through his thoughts like a silent ticker tape while he was motoring between towns or struggling with French irregular verbs in his hotel room. It set him fantasising about being scolded and chastised for poor work, and the more he imagined the sting of Estelle's ruler on his bottom, the more inflamed became his desire for the reality. Time and again he vowed to confess his longing on returning home, telling himself that his wife, mature woman that she was, would understand and satisfy. But always the conviction that his weakness was shameful and unmanly, buttressed by the fear that confession might be greeted with derision, held his tongue even when he deliberately loosened it with alcohol.

Envy of his stepson tempted Bruce to bring the conversation round to Estelle's treatment of him. He chose a Saturday morning when they were driving back to Hurworth from Chester. Monty was in the passenger seat, steadying Fiver, who was standing on his hind legs, his head sticking out of the half-open window, his eyes

97

streaming in the wind. Estelle was behind them at the wheel of her newly-acquired Vauxhall Cavalier.

'What do you fear most in life, Monty?' Cameron began. 'We all have a secret dread, don't we? With some people it's being offered a job, with others it's having to spend some money. Jack Hazelhurst tells a tale about a man known to his friends as Egg-nog. He was so mean that a small crowd would gather if word got round that he was about to spend a few pounds.'

'What do *you* fear most, Ibzy? You've had longer than I to develop complexes.'

'Noise. No question about it. Noise goes straight to my stomach. But back to you. Tell me your great dread. Being a castaway, like Robinson Crusoe? Going mad without knowing you're going mad? Being buried alive.'

'Being parted from Mama.'

'But, Monty, Mama spanks you!' Bruce protested, feigning perplexity.

'Perhaps I enjoy it. Perhaps I like what happens afterwards.'

'And what's that?'

'I'm not saying.'

'Come on! I can keep a secret.'

'Mama whispers in my ear that girls will cut it off.'

'She says that?'

'Don't say anything. She might stop.'

The worst punishment Estelle could inflict on her son was the denial of her goodnight kiss. Although a happy, mischievous boy, Monty had inherited not only Clyde's blond delicacy but also the nervous anxiety that was an expression of deep-seated insecurity. He had to have a night light burning in his room, and his door as well as the sitting room door had to be left ajar. The bed-wetting had stopped even before the move to Hurworth, but nightmares were frequent and only his mother, sitting on the edge of his bed, could soothe them away.

Considering the bruising indifference, even hostility, with which she sometimes made him miserable, Estelle was surprisingly patient and sympathetic in this respect, even when going to him meant leaving her bed in the small hours.

'My sister used to cane me,' Cameron lied, wanting to continue talk of beatings.

'Mama says you lost your mother and father in a house fire.'

'They had a fish and chip shop in Bayswater and we lived over it. Joan, my sister, had just married and I went to live with her and her husband. She was strict with me – hence the canings.'

'You didn't like them, Ibzy?'

'I did not.'

'I read in a book that in a boarding school here in England, the boys' name for beating was stimulation.'

Cameron's laugh was mirthless.

'All it stimulated in me was the desire to avoid a repetition,' he declared.

Monty turned round in his seat.

'Mama's still behind us. I thought we were going to lose her at those traffic lights,' he said. Having waved to her, he faced front again, smiling. His were strong, white teeth, one upper incisor very slightly overlapping its neighbour in a precise repeat of his mother's dental configuration.

'Mama's a smart businesswoman,' Cameron said, warmly approving. 'What did you think of her performance this morning, Monty?'

Estelle had decided the night before to change her car and Bruce thought it a good idea to change his at the same time. Following breakfast, the Camerons had prepared the two cars for the dealers, Estelle cleaning the interiors while Bruce and Monty washed and polished. Later, the two stood listening in amused admiration as

Estelle bargained with three dealers in succession, finally returning to the first to exchange her red Metro and to the third to trade Bruce's Maxi for a Ford Capri.

Cameron said: 'Estelle could run a corporation.'

Monty replied: 'She will one day, if only by remote control.'

'I don't know when I last watched a more charming and resolute negotiator.'

'She was like that when we went to buy my piano. Bunting was our technical adviser, but it was Mama who did the talking.'

'The iron hand inside the velvet glove, Monty.'

Not for the first time, Bruce wondered how much his reticent wife was worth in cash and investments. He knew from Clyde Beaumont that she was a major shareholder in the family business and his common sense told him that she had profited handsomely from Clyde's death. That she was a rich woman was confirmed by the regular meetings she had with her financial adviser. He clearly counted Estelle among his more important clients, since he visited her, not she him. Bruce had seen him only once, as he was leaving the bungalow, briefcase in hand, to return to his Bentley, and had been favoured with a curt nod. The visitor knew who had the money, recognised a rep when he saw one, and communicated with Cameron via Estelle when Bruce sought his advice on a taxation matter.

'Is this where you play squash, Ibzy?' Monty asked, when they were driving past a leisure centre that lay between Chester and Hurworth.

It was. Liking the boy's company and recalling Estelle's wishes, Bruce suggested joining him one day. 'You'll enjoy it, Monty. Or meet me at the clay shoot after Mass and count how many times I miss the target.'

Momentary silence and a faraway smile indicated that

Monty wasn't interested. He didn't think Mama would approve of shooting on the Sabbath.

'She lets me go,' Bruce reasoned.

'You're different. Mama says that lay-by we've just passed is where the secret policeman used to wait for you. You christened him Inspector Shy because he never approached you.'

'He led the Special Branch team who kept me under surveillance for a year or so after I'd written cocky letters to our dear Royal Family.'

'Mama says he just stared at you from the side window of his car.'

'The idea was to let me know that my telephone was being tapped as part of their security check and by way of discouraging me from sending more letters. Inspector Shy, listening in, would hear me making my appointments to play squash. He would then post himself in the lay-by and, okay, just stare at me.'

'It must have been creepy.'

'They had nothing on me that could bring them to my door.'

'Do you know what a corpse candle is, Ibzy?'

'Can't say I do.'

'It's a light that flickers over a grave after dark. That must be really creepy. Mama says Catholics don't believe in the supernatural. If we see anything, we make the sign of the cross and it will go away. How's your French coming along?'

'Mama hasn't smacked me yet.'

'Make the same mistake two or three times and stand by for action.'

'I'll remember that, Monty.'

'Will you get a job that takes you abroad once your French is up to scratch?'

'If Mama will let me.'

'As an export salesman perhaps?'

101

'Everything depends on Mama,' Cameron said. 'Like you, Monty, I do as I'm told.'

He checked in his rearview mirror that his wife was still on his tail, then turned his nearly-new black Capri into Sunnyside Gardens, which Monty had christened Suicide Gardens, and drove through the estate to the bungalow.

'Look who's waiting to welcome us home,' he muttered, displeased.

Unfazed, Monty exclaimed: 'The Terrible Trio! Mama won't tell them to clear off. She says if she did they'd only do it all the more.'

'Are they a nuisance when I'm away?'

'Sometimes. If they've got nothing better to do, they hang around outside and whistle after me when I take Fiver for his walk, or they play football in front of the sitting room windows. That's the part that annoys Mama.'

The boys moved a little to make way for Bruce's car. Once parked facing the garage, he handed his house key to his stepson and said reassuringly: 'You go on inside.'

Drifting away and grinning, the Trio jeered at Monty as he walked with his unusual, slightly slithering step to the front door. 'Sissy. Girly-boy. Where's your skirt, love?'

To Cameron's astonishment, Monty turned, key raised to the lock, to smile at the boys. It wasn't bravado. He was amused and flattered.

He went through to the conservatory to spend a few minutes on the exercise bike. Estelle followed her husband into the kitchen, where he filled the kettle to make coffee. No mention was made of the incident, but it started Estelle thinking afresh about her son's future. In a low voice, she confided: 'Monty must have realised at *Les Merles,* if not before, that there's money in the family, and he's the sort who could all too easily idle his life away. He must train for a career, Bruce. I won't have him turn into a rich playboy like your feeble Duke of Windsor.'

'He's a talented cook,' Cameron pointed out, smiling.

'My son is not going to be a *chef de cuisine.*'

'*Je vous demande pardon, madame.*'

'I've thought of the law, medicine, the priesthood; but prolonged and solitary study isn't Monty. So he's going to be a professional musician.'

'Have you told him yet?'

'Monty loves music. He has his radio in his room and now he wants me to let him have a record player. Bunty assures me he has keyboard talent. I'm going to see he develops it. My little cry-baby is going to work hard.'

Cameron took his wife in his arms, kissed her pretty nose and pressed his cheek to hers.

'You're the one to make him,' he murmured, swaying her a little. 'You and your ruler.'

'Will you do something for me, Bruce?'

'To hear is to obey.'

'Will you take a fertility test? It isn't me. If it's you, I've talked to my doctor and there is treatment available.'

3

Sitting in the sun lounge of the Racquets Club, with the bowling green to look at and the click-clack of snooker balls reaching them from the Games Room, Jack Hazelhurst asked Bruce what differences marriage had made to his life.

'Hardly any, apart from having a pretty wife to come home to and a stepson who makes me laugh,' Cameron replied. 'I expected Estelle to stamp her identity on my bungalow, but she hasn't.'

He kept from adding 'It's as if she's only passing

through', because the possibility of its being true disturbed and preoccupied him.

'We live together in harmony and peace,' he said, using a line from Masonic ritual to see if Jack was a Mason. No response. So Bruce added: 'Monty is easily excited, but Estelle's always serene and very easy to live with. She has a violent temper—'

'I've heard about that.'

'—but I've never seen it. If I have a complaint, Jack, it is that she never wants to go anywhere. Monty's the same. I'm on holiday all this week. I wanted the three of us to take a trip somewhere, but neither of them showed a spark of interest. I got them as far as Bayswater, where I grew up, but that's all.'

They had viewed from the road, sitting in the Ford Capri under drumming rain, the flat where Bruce had lived with his sister and her husband, Joan and Ray Wallace, in the years between his parents' death and the Wallaces' departure for Australia. These were the years that saw the end of his grammar school education, his five-year apprenticeship as a marine engineer at Cammell Laird's shipyard and, at age thirty, his decision to become what he then called a travelling salesman. He completed a correspondence course in salesmanship, bringing to it the same will to succeed as he was now applying to a management course and to his learning of French with Estelle.

Jack said: 'I had two shots at learning Spanish with records and text books, and the second time I stuck it to the bitter end. I was a bus driver with the Crosville, driving a Bristol Lodekker on the Birkenhead-Chester route. That's how I met Bunty. Have you ever driven a bus?'

'Never. Pretty boring, I should think.'

'Not at the time I was driving. No servo-assisted brakes in those days, no power-steering, no automatic

104

transmission. Skill, patience and elbow grease. But the Lodekker was a joy to drive. She was rock-solid – know what I mean? – and the engine produced a rich, rumbling sound. I thought if I learnt Spanish and maybe French or German later, I might get a job driving a coach with one of these tour companies; but by the end of the course, I could do no more than ask and answer simple questions, and even then I was so slow that life had moved on before I could get my words together. There's something missing in language learning, but I don't know what it is.'

'Complete immersion. That's what's lacking, in my opinion. The drawback with recorded language courses is that you learn the lessons as you would, say, a piano concerto. The fact that you've mastered the concerto doesn't mean you can sit down and play at sight any piece of music that's set before you. The student who hasn't been able to practise speaking the language with a native speaker can't easily converse or understand or even marshall enough words to do more than ask for a railway ticket.'

'I've found that to be true.'

'Estelle says you've got to be surrounded by the language day and night, seeing and hearing nothing except French and with no choice but to speak it,' Bruce concluded. 'I'm lucky. My wife won't let me speak English at home anymore. I make mistakes, okay, but the student who never made a mistake never got on top of a foreign language.'

'Some say intelligence is an impediment in language learning because brainy people are too self-critical,' Jack said. 'You've mentioned mistakes: they don't like making them. I knew a lad in the POW camp in Germany – a Scouser – with very little in the way of education; but he picked up German so quickly and so well that the commandant gave him a job in the Orderly Room – *die*

Schreibstube. If he never progressed beyond the present tense, if he got his verbs in the wrong place, that didn't bother him. He just ploughed ahead, dropping clangers with careless abandon, but the guards understood him and he understood them.'

'And that's all that matters, unless you're preparing for exams,' Cameron said. 'Even then, we should laugh at our blunders, the way children do, instead of taking them to heart.'

'Scouse, as we called this lad, stayed in Germany after the war and married a German girl. Changing the subject, what made you give up marine engineering?'

'Dirty clothes, dirty hands, dirty boots. I wanted a dress-up job so that I could go straight from work to a dance or to Peterkin's Gymnasium over in Liverpool.'

'But you could have gone to sea as an officer.'

'Don't like the sea, Jack. A country cousin, not very bright, seeing it for the first time, looked at it for several minutes and then asked 'Is this all it does?'. The sea is Nature's big bore.'

'You're quite an athlete, Bunty says. I'm the reverse. Do you still dance? You and Estelle.'

'Estelle won't come and she wouldn't let me go on my own,' Bruce replied, fantasising for a moment. 'She knits for St Mary's charity shop, Monty tickles the ivories and I'm more and more content to be just a family man. I've even dropped my Friday night riding lesson.'

'Still shooting?'

'I've just bought a new shotgun – well, second hand. I'm learning new tricks from my dear wife. It's a Sable Gunmark, side-by-side, twenty-eight inch barrels.'

Unlike Jack and Bunty Hazelhurst, the Camerons were not addicted television viewers. The bungalow had been without a receiver until Estelle brought hers from Oildrum Court together with personal effects and the little presents Monty had given her from time to time.

With the money from the sale of Clyde's Jensen, repaired and repainted, she had bought Monty's piano, as well as saleroom furniture for his bedroom.

Unexpectedly, Estelle, who couldn't bear to be idle, was of help to Bruce in his work. Sitting in the office, she collated his business expenses for submission to the three manufacturers he represented, checked his bank statements to see that his retainers and commission were being paid and completed his tax returns. His customers praised her pleasing manners (evident in Monty too), some of them admitting to finding reasons for telephoning Hurworth so as to hear her calming voice with its educated Canadian accent. At trade receptions and Masonic half-nights, smiling and beautifully dressed, she made Bruce proud to introduce her as Mrs Cameron.

'You're a man who knows where he's going and what he wants from life, and you're to be envied,' Jack told him. 'I lost my bearings when the public decided they didn't want Sunny Picket anymore. Do you know about my stage and screen career – how brief it was, how little joy it brought me?'

'I know you rarely mention it.'

Jack said he loosened up after his third whisky, becoming almost human.

'It left me very bitter when it petered out,' he went on. 'At first, I was mad at my father for squandering my fortune while I was behind the wire, but later I discovered he hadn't spent it all on himself and his women. He'd been lending money to right, left and centre. You'll never be short of friends, you know, when you've got money. Before the war, when I was raking it in, all sorts of johnnies thought I should help them. They expected me to clear their mortgage, buy them a car or a hairdressing business or send them to Swiss clinics for convalescence; and because I was a minor, my father was signing cheques on my behalf. He trusted these people to pay him back, and most, even blood relatives, betrayed him.'

Reluctant to accept that he would never again be a star, Jack had lingered on the fringe of the entertainment world for several years after the Second World War, doing menial work for a living while getting walk-on parts in plays and films, appearing in magazine and television advertisements and waiting for the breakthrough into adult roles that never came.

'Eventually, I faced reality. A play I was in that had done well in London flopped in Liverpool, leaving me without my fare home. I got a job as a bus conductor with Birkenhead Corporation, then as a driver with Crosville, based first at West Kirby, then at Chester. But I'd started drinking heavily and it lost me my licence. I was back to low-paid work – groundsman at a golf links, window cleaning, labourer on a building site – living in a bedsit till I found rats in my food cupboard one night, then in a hostel. I was close to suicide when I walked into St Mary's Church one summer evening and met my saviour.'

Bunty had been assisting Father Coglan in the laying-on of hands. Jack was seeking relief from the intermittent muscular contraction in his neck that doctors had assured him was imaginary, but which, when it occurred, pressed on the windpipe so that he felt he was choking. When he and Bruce were talking about it at the Racquets Club, Jack had been untroubled by it for some weeks.

'But it has returned, with touching loyalty, and is worse than I've known it. With reluctance, I may have to go to the doctor again and be told it's all in the mind because, being a soft tissue injury, it doesn't show on an X-ray – like, I believe, the prostate gland.'

'Have you tried Chinese medical treatment?' Bruce asked, lighting his pipe.

Jack shook his head. Bruce suggested that acupuncture might help Jack towards a cure, combined perhaps with herbal medication. Western medicine, he maintained, treated symptoms, not causes, and he quoted Voltaire's dictum: Medicine amuses the patient while Nature cures the disease.

Jack gave a single bark of sardonic laughter. Bruce had noticed and so had Estelle that he seldom laughed and was one of those people who almost never address us by name.

'Throw physic to the dogs!' he exclaimed, quoting Macbeth after his wife had gone mad. 'But there's no cure, Western or Eastern, for cancer, except surgery and even that can't be counted on to do the trick.'

'Who said you've got cancer?'

'Just a hunch of mine. Don't say anything to Estelle. You know how close the girls are. Have another drink – whisky – you're on holiday – and tell me about this London job you've written after.'

'The company is Blanchard Brothers, shotgun manufacturers. Not in the same league as Purdey or Holland & Holland, but they ran them a close third until they decided to stop making bespoke guns. A matched pair of Blanchard Supremes in good order still fetches a hefty price at auctions and house sales, but today the company just makes ready-to-fire shotguns – the Blanchard Standard.'

'I don't expect there are many people left who can afford thousands of pounds for made-to-measure guns.'

'They were bought mostly by the landed gentry.'

'The folk who went north for the shooting, while the likes of me went south for the drinking. I ought to smoke a pipe, like you. I've concluded too late in life that cigarettes aren't good for me.'

'I found they slowed me down,' Bruce said. 'When I lit the first one in the morning, it was as if someone had hung weights from my shoulders.'

109

'Bunty's always at me to chuck it. In a nice way, you understand. Bunty doesn't nag. Does Estelle?'.

'Never. She just tells me what to do and I do it. I gave up cigarettes because I had a brother-in-law, Ray Wallace, who was always cadging them off me. He was a decent sort, but a scrounger and a monumental bore.'

In Bayswater days, Bruce told Jack, Ray had been a motor mechanic at a garage in Liverpool. When Bruce thought of him, he saw him at the fireside in Wellingtons and a blue boiler suit so matted with oil as to appear almost black. He wore horn-rimmed spectacles and often a leather fingerstall. Smiling at his memories, he never wearied of regaling anyone who would listen with tales of his war exploits in the Royal Army Service Corps – tales which became longer, slower and more elaborate with each telling. Some of his personal possessions, past and present, were, he claimed, unique: one item might have been a traveller's sample, another the prototype of an article that never went into production, whilst a third might have been for export only or made specifically for someone who passed away before taking delivery. Mention beer and Ray would tell you where to find the best bitter in England: mention the hottest summer you can remember and Ray would recall an even hotter one.

'He had a habit of calling me son,' Bruce revealed, 'which annoyed me, so I retaliated by just calling him Wallace, which I knew he didn't like.'

Ruefully, Jack said: 'I call Monty son.'

'That's not the same thing.'

'His smiling face brightens our lives. He larks around so much, doing impersonations and suchlike, that Bunty has to say to him "Hey! Remember you're here to learn, Scamp".'

Mrs Macdonald at End Point and the Hazelhursts were not alone in saying they wanted to adopt Monty Cameron. Throughout his life, his prettiness and bracing optimism, his endearing laughter and cut-and-come-again gaiety, would win the affection, even adoration, of men as well as women. Those captivated by his epicene charm were initially responding to what was childish in him. Later, when it dawned on them that he was a fairy, women became protective, whilst the knowing leers of men slowly lapsed into acceptance of his deviant sexuality, with only the occasional barb or innuendo to indicate contempt or inflate their self-esteem.

'Ray had all sorts of off-beat theories,' Bruce said. 'He insisted that it should be possible to arrange colours in various combinations to make the onlooker feel sad or happy, eager or lethargic.'

'I was thinking the other day that if sharps were printed in red and flats in blue, that would make them easier to identify,' Jack said. 'Music scores have other indications, all of them printed in black on white paper. They'd be so much easier to read, to anticipate, if they were printed in a variety of colours. Am I drunk or mad?'

'Both. I'm sure Ray found me just as tedious as I found him. Or was he too self-absorbed?' Cameron wondered. 'My sister sometimes told me that it was me who talked too much, and always about sport or politics. Joan was a barmaid. She had gone to work by the time Ray and I came home, leaving our evening meal ready in the oven.'

'No children?'

'No. They were saving for a house and to start their own business, with Joan serving petrol on the forecourt while Ray did the servicing and repairs. Now they've got both, but in Tasmania instead of in the County Borough of Bayswater. Joan wants to meet Estelle one day and Monty too. So far they've only talked over the phone.'

'How do they feel about living in London? – Estelle and Scamp, I mean.'

'Estelle says we'll talk about that if I'm offered the job. I know she's not enthusiastic about city life. Chester is just the right size for her.'

The vacancy at Blanchard Brothers was for a sales manager/director designate and would involve appointing and supervising agents in Britain and France, where Blanchard guns, perhaps because of their French-sounding name, had traditionally sold well through outlets in Paris and Marseille.

'What does Monty say about London?' Jack asked. 'Is he excited?'

'Monty's a puzzle. He bounces round like a rubber ball, yet shows no interest in anything outside the home apart from looking after horses. You'd expect a boy to ask what make of car Blanchard's would provide, whereabouts in London we would live, how many times a year I'd go to France and could he come with me. Instead, his only question about London, believe it or not, is where the Monseigneur nightclub was located. I've never heard of it. Have you, Jack?'

'Let's have a game of snooker while there's a table free and I'll tell you what little I know about the place.'

Chapter Six

When they were first married, Cameron had telephoned
Estelle every Wednesday evening from his hotel to ask if
she and Monty were all right. But gradually, discouraged
by her easy indifference, he had dropped the habit, only
to feel yet more bruised when she failed to remark its
termination. Then came an evening when she called him.
He thought she was about to pass on a message from one
of his customers, but no: Estelle was pregnant.

'At least, I think so, Bruce. I've never gone as long as
this before.'

She was jubilant. Her fingers were crossed, she said,
and she was asking God to send her a little girl.

'There's a letter for you, Ibzy, from these Blanchard
Brothers. They want to see you in London next
Thursday, the twenty-fifth. So teeth in, curlers out and
best foot forward.'

'Will you let me take Scamp with me?'

'Anyone can do anything now,' Estelle replied, laughing.

'I know it's no good asking if you'll come too.'

'I'll see you Friday, darling. And thank you.'

Sitting on the side of his bed, Cameron slowly
replaced the receiver and stayed looking at it while
sipping a little of the whisky that was always his trav-

elling companion. He had never been in love with Estelle, only with the ideal she embodied of the ultra feminine woman who beat her husband. Should her dearest wish be granted, the possibility of his being fulfilled would recede yet further. Estelle's absorption with her Dawnia would make her even less mindful of Bruce than at present.

He would have to be content, it seemed, with the pleasure of her company, both in and out of bed, and adjust to parenthood. Before drifting into sleep, he decided that being father to his own child might prove energising and gratifying, strengthening rather than weakening the bond between himself and Estelle. He saw himself standing at her side, his arm round her waist, she with the adored baby in her arms, smiling fondly down and then with almost equal fondness at Bruce, as though to say: 'We did this together.'

By lunchtime next day, when dialling his Hurworth number, he was starting to look forward to the adventure of parenting and to the possibility that a loving relationship might purge him of the unwholesome desires which had, in his bachelor years, been fuelled and relieved by the erotic literature that he had destroyed on the eve of his marriage.

Because Estelle always answered the telephone by announcing 861112, Cameron thought he had misdialled when a female voice said, very softly, as if in the presence of the dead: 'Hello?'

'Estelle?' he prompted, frowning.

'It's Bunty, Brian. Estelle's at the dressmaker's.'

'Well, what are you doing in my home?' Bruce demanded.

'Estelle asked me to stay a little while with Monty.'

'Put him on.'

'He's resting in his room, Brian.'

Bruce shouted: 'I said put him on.'

114

'I can't. His door is locked and his mother has the key with her. Is there nothing I can do?'

Infuriated, Cameron slammed the receiver down. The following evening, when he let himself into the bungalow, Estelle, unsmiling, came out of the kitchen and into his arms.

'Well?' he murmured into her ear.

'No,' she whispered. 'We'll just have to keep on trying.'

'Is Monty all right?'

'Monty's fine.'

'What happened yesterday?'

'I'd rather not talk about it.'

'Why the mystery?'

'Let's just say it was something between my son and me.'

Estelle was subdued, preoccupied, saying little until the weekend call came through from Quebec. She took it on the bedroom extension, perched on the edge of the double divan, and Bruce, in the room with her, understood most of what she was saying. She talked business with her father, then her mother came on the line and Estelle lowered her voice and gestured to Cameron to close the door. He recognised the noun *règles* as the French for periods, then the subject changed to a pending *intervention chirurgicale*.

Watching and listening, he wondered yet again why his wife had never invited him to speak with her parents and why, apparently, they had never asked to be introduced. His occupation had probably satisfied them that he was *petit bourgeois* and therefore an unsuitable match for their daughter; another feasible explanation being Louis de Champêtre's dislike of the British. His resentment of the Monarchy and of Whitehall influence over Canadian affairs were minor issues compared with the loss of his brother, a subaltern in the Canadian army, killed in an abortive raid on Dieppe early in the Second World War. He understood that the raid had been staged because Canadian troops stationed in southern England were idle and becoming mutinous. Of the five thousand men put ashore from landing craft, nearly one thousand were killed and more than two thousand taken prisoner by the Germans.

'Bad news?' Bruce asked, when Estelle gently replaced the handset.

She nodded, was silent for a moment, then began to cry, almost soundlessly, her hands covering her face.

Sitting down next to her, Bruce put his arm round her shoulders and asked what was wrong. He had never seen her cry before.

'My mother has got to have one of her feet amputated. Poor soul!' she whispered. 'Hasn't she suffered enough?'

Monty tapped discreetly on the door.

'Mama? Mama, are you all right, Mama?'

Estelle, dabbing her eyes, said: 'I'm fine, dear. Ibzy and I are only talking. Let me hear you begin your practice, Monty. It's eight o'clock.'

'Yes, Mama.'

Estelle waited, then said quietly that she might go to Canada, just for a few days.

'I shall miss you,' Bruce said, 'even for a few hours.'

She took his free hand in both of hers and told him, smiling: 'My toad will be all right on his own. It'll be quite like old times for you.'

Husband and wife were about equal in catering ability and household management, being competent if uninspired. Cameron had done everything for himself before marriage, whilst Estelle, living at *Les Merles,* had never so much as straightened a cushion. Cooking, cleaning, washing and ironing had all to be learnt when she arrived in England with Clyde Beaumont. Her son was now overtaking her, especially in the kitchen, making her suspect that he was consciously competing with her. His increasing domesticity, never more irritating than when he roguishly seized her latest *Woman & Home* with the cry 'Me first,' sometimes brought her close to rounding on him. Checked by the awareness that he couldn't help being as he was, she told herself that coaxing was the most humane way to bring about change. But did she in her heart want to change him? Estelle closed her mind to the truth that while Monty was what he was, a mother's boy, he would continue to belong to her.

Bruce asked if she would take Monty with her to Canada.

She was unsure.

'I'll see. He's still too young to be left here on his own.'

'He could come with me.'

'I might be gone a month, Ibzy. I don't suppose you'd take kindly to Bunty and Jack staying here? No, I didn't think you would,' Estelle said, with a smile. 'In that case, I'll take my cry-baby with me.'

But by next day, when they were sitting together in the social club after hacking at End Point, she had decided against going.

'My being there can't change anything, Bruce.'

'Why don't we have a few days' trail riding from Jedburgh?' he asked. 'Monty could take root at the Retreat House with your friend and her putative husband, Fiver could stay with the Bushells as before.'

'You'll never be reconciled to Bunty, will you?'

'You know, don't you, that she's charging more than the standard rate for these piano lessons she's giving Monty?'

'I'm surprised, Bruce, that you took it upon yourself to check. Surprised and a little displeased.'

'I'm only thinking of you and Monty. She's not a

professional. How do you know she's capable of preparing him for examinations?'

'Be a dear, Ibzy, and leave me to do the worrying. Okay?'

Estelle pushed aside soft brown hair that had strayed over one eye, tilted her head a little and smiled at her husband.

'Will you do something for me?' she asked.

'Anything.'

'When you're in London next week with Monty, will you have a little talk with him? It's time he caught up with the birds and the bees.'

2

They stayed at the Eccleston Hotel, only a short walk from London Victoria. After dinner on their last evening, Cameron asked his stepson why Estelle had shut him in his room on the previous Thursday. The boy's voice, normally lively and sometimes loud enough to earn a maternal rebuke, fell to an awed whisper when he replied that she had beaten him in his room before leaving him and locking his door.

'It was terrible, Ibzy. I'd seen her clobber my father, but it was the first time she'd done it to me. She'd been in a foul mood all morning.'

Cameron could guess why. He asked if Bunty Hazelhurst had been present during the beating.

Monty shook his head.

'She came after Mama had shut me away.'

'How often does she come to Suicide Gardens, Monty?'

'Most days. She turns up on her scooter after she's finished her postal round. My lessons with Mama are over by then. Mama makes tea or coffee and the three of us sit talking.'

Bruce and Monty were seated in a corner of the hotel lounge with a low table separating their leather armchairs. Their drinks and a glass ashtray stood on the table, also a pink-shaded lamp. In its soft glow, Monty's facial skin had the colour and texture of a peach.

Lighting his pipe and feigning only casual interest, Bruce asked the boy why Estelle had beaten and imprisoned him. Monty lowered his gaze to answer huskily: 'She caught me doing something. It was the breaking point. She'd been beastly to me since breakfast. Mama can be unbearable at times, Ibzy.'

He started crying – quietly, unobtrusively, the way Estelle had cried, and it was over just as quickly.

Bruce said: 'You say she caught you, as though what you were doing is a crime.'

'Mama says it's sinful. She made me confess it to Father Coglan on Saturday night. I'm never to do it again. If she catches me, I'm for it.'

'It can happen when you're asleep.'

'That's what I'm dreading.'

'I'll talk to her. As a matter of fact, she has asked me to tell you the facts of life.'

'I've already heard them from the girls at End Point Riding Centre. They make sport of me, but I like it. They tickle me till I'm sick with laughter. In the tack room last Sunday, when you and Mama were out with the two o'clock hack, one of them pinned my arms behind my back and another pulled my pants down while the rest pointed at me and laughed themselves silly.'

'They won't find debagging you quite so easy now that you're wearing long trousers with braces instead of a belt .'

The three Camerons had gone to a Chester outfitter's to buy the twopiece single-breasted suit that Monty was now wearing. It was the cheapest on the rail, Estelle explaining to the salesman that her son, already tall for his age, would soon grow out of it.

'Mama won't let me wear it at home. I like the pretty pattern, don't you? Bunting calls it Prince of Wales check.'

'Named after the parasite who became Duke of Windsor,' Bruce said. One of his letters to the Queen had been prompted by his outrage at the discovery that Windsor had been willing to attend almost any social gathering in return for a cheque for five thousand US dollars.

'The man was taking backhanders,' Bruce had told his delighted wife. 'In addition of course to being kept in luxury by the British taxpayer.'

'Oh, I must tell Papa this! Old Isoscelys will rejoice in passing it on to his cronies at the golf club,' Estelle had responded.

'Tell him something else about Windsor. He can use it as an encore. Tell him that the craven weakling, the little coward who dodged out of his moral responsibilites, spent the Second World War in the Bahamas with his woman, enjoying sunshine and the best of everything while our Nation fought for its life.'

In contrast to Monty's check, Bruce was wearing the plain grey suit he had worn for his interview with Blanchard's earlier that day. Smoothing his lapels before he set out from Hurworth, Estelle had assured him that mid-grey was his colour. 'Dark clothes make us look older than we are, Ibzy, and there is already a hint of silver in your tough black hair' – just at the temples, where the ladies like to see it. Grey suit, black eyes, silver tie, and such a torso inside that crisp white shirt!'

She wasn't lying. Above and below the pinched waist, Cameron's body carried not an ounce of unnecessary flesh. His biceps bulged under tension, whilst his back was a lattice of rippling muscles and his chest seemed formed of two panels of dense tissue. He could have made a living posing for photographs in men's 'health' magazines.

'Mmm ... My man is all man,' Estelle was fond of crooning. This time, she had added: 'Don't forget to come back to me and with your batteries fully charged.'

While Bruce was being interviewed, Monty had waited in Blanchard's showroom, taking not the least interest in the polished shotguns lining the walls or the boxed cartridges stacked in a fixture behind the manager's desk. Instead, he faced the plate glass windows, one to each side of the street door, watching with fascination the owners of luxury cars entering and leaving Brown's Hotel. Money didn't matter to him, but elegance did, and its fullest expression, he had decided, was to be found in the West End night clubs of the 1930s. In his room at Hurworth, with the door closed to keep from disturbing Mama and Ibzy, he played over and over the LP he had recently bought of dance music recorded by Roy Fox's band during its residency at the Monseigneur night club only a few paces away from Piccadilly Circus.

'Where will we live, Ibzy, if you bag this wonderful job?' Monty asked, after Bruce had ordered their last drinks at the Eccleston. 'To my undisguised shame, cities being centres of Babylonian wickedness, I've fallen head over heels in love with London.'

'There's a flat above Blanchard's showroom. If they want me for a further interview, you and Mama will have to come here with me to look it over. For the time being, I'm short-listed.'

After Harrods, where the bedazzled boy had wanted to spend all day choosing a present for Mama, Bruce had treated Monty to afternoon tea at Fortnum & Mason's and dinner at L'Escargot. There wasn't time to visit Madame Tussaud's, the Tower of London or the Houses of Parliament and Monty didn't want to see them anyway; but he couldn't wait to watch a performance of *Swan Lake* at Covent Garden. Ballet was a new experience for him, and he sat motionless and a little forward in his seat, entranced by the scenery, the music, and especially the dancers. Throughout the performance, he was adrift in paradise, so completely severed from his surroundings as to forget to clap until reminded by the general applause. What was significant for his stepfather was his fixation with the principal male dancer – a tall and obvious homosexual whose skin-tight costume of shimmering silk accentuated crack and cluster.

Cameron found the boy's interest disturbing, even distasteful, but had the sense to ask himself why he did and to say to Monty when they were driving home next day: 'Forget any nonsense you've heard, even from Mama, about sex being dirty or wicked. Any sexual act that doesn't involve a minor or an unwilling partner, any act that doesn't hurt anyone – unless of course that person wants to be hurt – is clean and wholesome and completely divorced from sin. There are men who like other men, just as there are women who like other women. That's okay. There are men and women, boys and girls, who make love to each other without being married. That's okay too. But they should get married when the woman becomes pregnant if they haven't done so before, because children need a mother and a father in a loving and stable relationship. Do you understand what I'm saying?'

'Every word.'

'There are, I believe, men who want to be ill-treated by women, even punished like naughty boys. Such men ought not to feel guilty or ashamed of their desires. You say you enjoy being spanked by Mama and you don't feel guilt or shame or embarrassment over it. That's as it should be, Monty.'

'It's going to end, Ibzy, and I don't want it to. I don't

want to grow up. I want Mama and me to stay as we are now and never be separated.'

'That may be a little difficult to arrange. Incidentally, you haven't said what she did to you last Thursday,' Bruce said, as though suddenly remembering.

He was seeking titillation.

Monty said: 'She knocked me about.'

'A bit different from lying over her knee with your pants down, eh?'

'She pulled me off the bed and slammed me against the wall. I've never seen Mama in such a bitter rage. I don't know how many times she slapped me.'

'Perhaps she'll do the same to me one day, Monty. Perish the thought!'

'Mama won't hit you.'

'She beat your father.'

'That was different. Mama respects you.'

The comment prompted Cameron to reflect with mortification on the childishness, the absurdity, the hopelessness of his quest for chastisement and humiliation. In reflective mood, Estelle had recently told him of her occasional suspicion that she was a disappointment to him, that something was lacking. 'Is there? Tell me if there is, Bruce.' But even then the man whom she sometimes called Tarzan or Mr Muscles, this man who was so proud of his hirsute masculinity, could not admit that he wanted his wife to shout abuse at him, to spit in his face and slap and thump him till she had him on his knees, embracing her thighs and begging for mercy. She had to want to ill-treat him, just as he had to pretend that ill-treatment was the last thing he wanted. His experience with the prostitute had taught him that domination and violence had to be spontaneous, not requested, if they were to stimulate and satisfy.

It was late in the afternoon when Bruce and his stepson reached Suicide Gardens. The Terrible Trio were not in evidence, but Bunty's scooter was, standing in the middle of the drive and so obliging Cameron to park at the kerbside.

'You're early, you men,' Estelle began, meeting them in the hall with a welcoming smile.

A flustered Bunty bustled out of the sitting room, looking, Cameron thought, ridiculous in her crash helmet and overlong jacket. She said: 'I was just about to go, Brian.'

'Bruce,' Estelle corrected, pleasantly.

'Bruce!' Bunty exclaimed, tut-tutting. 'I'll get it right one day.'

Monty, already at his mother's side and with his arm round her, said happily: 'Bunting, tell Jack we found the site of the Monseigneur night club. It's now a cinema, would you believe?'

'Jack's got a photograph for you,' Bunty told the boy. 'Taken, he says, in nineteen thirty-one. It's an interior view of the club, showing couples dancing and Roy Fox playing the trumpet in front of his band.'

'Oh, I can't wait to see it!' Monty declared. 'We could have a print of it made, couldn't we, Mama?'

'It's for you to keep,' said Bunty. 'Jack found it in amongst his cuttings and playbills. Take it home with you after your next piano lesson.'

She edged past Bruce without looking at him, said goodbye to Estelle and was gone, leaving the subject of Monty's keyboard progress to be touched on again when he was asleep and Estelle and Bruce were undressing in the next room.

'Has your friend said anything more about examinations?' Cameron asked.

'Bunty? She's finding out if it's possible to take pianoforte as a GCSE subject. She thinks it is.'

'Well, she can save her short legs because I've found the real thing. The Associated Board of the Royal

124

Schools of Music offers exams to suit all levels of competence. I called at their premises in London.'

'Go on.'

'I've got a copy of their prospectus in the car. I meant to bring it in.'

'I should think it's exactly what Bunty's looking for, my toad.'

'Read it yourself first, Estelle. I think you'll be as surprised as I was. There's much more to music than I ever imagined. It's a whole new language with a vocabulary all its own,' Cameron said.

He got into bed with his wife and switched off the bedside lamp.

'There's nothing shameful,' he said, quietly, 'in what you found Monty doing.'

'He told you.'

'Only because I asked him why you locked him in his room.'

'I shouldn't have behaved as I did. I was overwrought and you can guess why. I've done all I can to make it up to him.'

'What he did, Estelle, is what every boy does. Some men continue it after marriage. Even your priests are not exempt.'

'I can't believe that.'

'You mean you won't.'

'Neither of us can possibly know.'

'Remember what you told me once about sexual pressure, Estelle? We all contain it, you said, and we all have to get rid of it. Your priests, sworn to the ridiculous rule of celibacy, are either playing with themselves or, worse, with children.'

'I don't like what you're saying, Ibzy.'

'That doesn't make it any less true. You've only to read the papers or listen to the radio.'

'The sexual energy of nuns and priests is sublimated to the service of God.'

'You may be right about nuns, Estelle, because women don't play with themselves to the extent that men do. Females have to be stimulated by touch or words or both, whereas males are aroused very easily by the imagination. What is the lightest thing on earth, Estelle?'

'I'm sure you have the answer to that as you have to everything else.'

'The penis. Even a thought can raise it. Which is why you must be sympathetic to your son. I had a little chat with him, by the way.'

'Thank you.'

'He knows more than we do.'

'End Point?'

'Top marks. I've drummed it into him that there is no sin in sex. Even homosexuality is acceptable provided it isn't paraded or forced on unwilling partners. The umbilical cord hasn't been cut in Monty's case, as I'm sure you've noticed.'

'Every day.'

'It may never be, and there's nothing shameful or wicked or unhealthy in that. There are men, Estelle, who remain mothers' boys all their lives, usually in secret because they don't want their wives to know that they want to be pampered, even punished, even made to wear short pants. What do you say to that?'

'I say it's time we forgot sex and made love instead.'

3

While Bruce and Estelle Cameron were trail riding from Jedburgh, Monty was spending a week at the Retreat House with Bunty and Jack Hazelhurst. In addition to paying for the trio's board and lodging, Estelle had provided cash for excursions with Monty and her Vauxhall Cavalier for Jack to drive.

'Before your praise gets too lavish,' he warned Bunty, 'consider what the Camerons are getting for their money – or I should say Estelle, because she decides what they spend.'

'Brian likes it that way apparently.'

'Bruce. You wouldn't get food and accommodation in a hotel at these prices. Lending us the car does away with taxi fares.'

Bunty went immediately on the defensive, pointing out that it was still a free holiday for her and Jack, and Monty was no trouble at all. As always, she would no more hear a word against Estelle than Estelle would against her.

Before the holiday, the two women had studied the Examination Syllabus of the Associated Board of the Royal Schools of Music over coffee and biscuits at Hurworth – Bunty with a sinking heart, Estelle with growing surprise at the discovery that music was not just a series of crochets and quavers, sharps and flats, but a complex arrangement of key and time-signatures, octave signs and grace notes.

'I don't know how you understand all this, Bunty,' she had said, turning to look in awe at her companion.

'I have to if I'm to teach,' Bunty had replied, clearing a dry throat and swallowing hard on the fact that the examination requirements went way beyond her competence. She was music's equivalent of the untrained language teacher who, ignorant of its grammatical substructure, can only teach students to speak and understand her native tongue. Bunty read music with difficulty and had no knowledge of pitch or accent marks. She was teaching Monty to play by ear, albeit with the appropriate sheet music propped up in front of him, which was how she had mastered the simple pieces required of her at St Mary's Church.

Humbled, she told Jack: 'I never thought his playing

127

would amount to anything more than a pastime', though without admitting her limitations.

But Estelle detected them, as she did the anxiety they were causing. After sleeping on it, she suggested Monty sit the Grade One examination rather than the higher grade that had been her first choice.

'With all the tuition you're giving him, Bunty, he should sail through,' she said, coming in with the morning coffee. 'Righty?'

Bunty, seated, with the Syllabus open in her lap, gave Estelle a pained, upward-slanting look and replied: 'Well, it won't be my fault if he doesn't. The teacher provides the spade: the student does the digging.'

But the knowledge that it would be her fault spurred her to do all she could to improve her teaching ability, including seeking advice and explanations from a violinist who played in amateur orchestras and sang in the choir at St Mary's. Estelle helped with the gift of *A Dictionary of Music*, bought for a few pence at a flea market in Frodsham, and by increasing the hour-long lessons to two a week.

'Her idea or yours?' Cameron asked, cynically, when they, along with other riders from the Jedburgh stables, were watering their horses at a stream in the Cheviot Hills.

'Mine,' his wife lied.

Bunty was tempted time and again to confess her inadequacy to Estelle and to suggest finding a qualified teacher. But the mounting difficulties of supporting herself and her feckless partner continued to silence her. She never told him that she often had to go over his well-intentioned but incompetent housework or that she was sometimes obliged to borrow money to meet such recurring expenses as shoe repairs and dry-cleaning or to provide extra comforts and little delicacies for the loved who, she now knew, was dying of throat cancer. What she was spared was the knowledge that he was mixing painkillers with whisky to try to dull the pain.

Monty was too fastidious ever to develop into an alcoholic, but he resembled Jack in being an incurable spendthrift with little understanding of the value of money and still less of its management. Estelle had started giving him pocket money, then stopped when she saw that he was spending most of it on her. 'Don't deny me my pleasure, Mama' he would say, when remonstrated with for bringing her chocolates or a nosegay. Nowadays, he had to tell her what he wanted money for before she would give him any.

'Estelle is more French than Canadian,' Jack observed, rubbing thumb and forefinger together for Bunty's delectation. Estelle's thrift tickled rather than displeased him. 'Have you seen that record player she bought, Cock? It's twenty years old if it's a day.'

'Monty has pasted the Roy Fox photo you gave him into the lid. Estelle is careful, I'll grant you that, but not mean. When she handed me a hundred pounds to spend on Monty, she insisted she doesn't want no receipts.'

'I should hope she doesn't!' Jack exclaimed, his dignity punctured. 'For two pints, I'd put the money on a horse. I haven't been so insulted since that fellow at the club had the sauce to tell me I don't know everything.'

'Remember, beloved, it's tomorrow night we're taking Scamp to the ballet in Manchester. Don't have a drink before we go, will you? Save it till we are all three safely back here.'

The Hazelhursts had already taken the boy to watch motor racing at Oulton Park and to marvel at the exquisitely decorated and sumptuously furnished Tatton Hall. 'I adore luxury, don't you, Bunting?' he had declared. 'Who was it said he could do without the necessities of life so long as he had its luxuries? Quite frankly, as you would say, I'm spellbound and itching to move in with Mama right away.'

Monty's enthusiasms, intense and joyful, were as contagious as his mirth. Except for morning lessons with his mother, when he had to keep a straight face, he turned everything to laughter. A born actor, he delighted in an audience. After hearing him sing Noel Coward songs with the composer's clipped diction, recite limericks and do an imitation of Old Isoscelys that owed a little to Grumpy in Disney's masterpiece, Jack, smiling and clapping, called him a one-man cabaret. Bunty didn't like his poking fun at Pope John Paul, calling him a senile transvestite, and she turned her face away in exaggerated disgust when he repeated Bruce Cameron's assertion that the Pope had ceased to claim infallibility after buying a ticket for the Irish Sweep and losing. Bunty disliked 'that Brian' for no better reason than that he disliked and patently mistrusted her.

'Cameron only married Estelle for her money,' she told Jack, when they were alone in the Green Room, which was the only area in the Retreat House where smoking was permitted. 'And now, if he gets this London job, he'll take her from us. Monty too. Have you ever heard of these Blanchard Brothers? Does anyone know anything about them? Scamp says nobody came in to buy nothing while he was waiting for Cameron to come out of the interview room.'

Jack noiselessly refilled his tumbler with Bell's Scotch Whisky, then returned the bottle to its hiding place down beside his armchair. Alcohol was forbidden everywhere within the boundaries of Stanmore Abbey.

Many years before meeting Bunty, he had been to Blanchard's showroom in Albemarle Street with the actor/manager Clive Valance.

'Val, we used to call him, because he thought Clive sounded too solemn. He was pally with Max Blanchard, who ran the sales and administrative side of the business, while Max's brother, who I think was called Simon, was the technical director based at the factory in Cricklewood. The Blanchards owned a few hundred acres of shooting at a village called Arrowcross in Hampshire, or maybe in wild Wilts, and Val sometimes joined them there.'

Jack recalled the atmosphere in the showroom, so quiet yet so close to Piccadilly, the display of burnished shot-guns, some with barrels of Damascus steel, which reminded him now of Bunty's lower legs, blotched from too much sitting over the fire, and the stacks of boxed cartridges, the boxes differing in colour according to manufacturer, bore and size of shot. A heavy Wilton carpet bearing a pattern of game birds on a khaki ground, specially designed and woven by Elkington's of Wolverhampton, covered the expanse of floor.

Unlike Clive Valance, Bruce Cameron had neither the desire nor the means to be a member of a game shoot. In his mid-forties now, he ignored but no longer scorned the class of men who indulged in blood sports, grouping and dismissing them with the lesser breed of social excluders who could afford no greater distinction than their own pewter tankard at the Racquets Club. 'Short of fouling the pavement, that's the only way they can get them-selves noticed,' he told Estelle.

Prompted by Monty's example, he had started reading again, usually in bed at his hotel after squash and a leisurely dinner. Detective fiction had replaced the politi-cal writings that had once fed his Socialism and fired his trades union activities. Marriage had mellowed him.

'I like Bruce,' Jack told Bunty. 'He's on the level. I want him to join the Club, but he says his wife won't let him.'

'Estelle? Don't believe him!'

'He may have been joking.'

'Quite frankly, Estelle doesn't give a hoot where Cameron goes or what he does when he gets there. Cameron's hiding something, Jack. I sensed it right from the start. You've got to dislike someone to see deeply into them.'

'What is he hiding?'

'I don't know and I don't care. He's good to Monty and good for him – I'll say that much for the man. They spend a lot of time together.'

Not growing up among children of his own age had made Monty older than his years. This maturity, allied to good manners and his facility for sharing the feelings of others, made him receptive and stimulating company. He liked to talk, but he was too an attentive listener, especially to Jack's stories of the London theatre and of the feature films he had made at the Teddington studios in the 1930s. Bunty rejoiced at the ease with which man and boy conversed as equals and the discovery that Monty was able to get her chap recalling without bitterness his blighted acting career. No one else in her experience had ever induced him to bring out of storage albums and scrapbooks covering his years as Sunny Picket.

'Scamp is as gentle as a girl,' she had said, smiling her approval. Monty had overheard the comment and was not offended. He needed neither The Terrible Trio nor the naughty-eyed girls at End Point Riding Centre to tell him he was more female than male. He knew it, was pleased about it and, in later life, would flaunt it. People noticed his habit of standing with crossed ankles and an index finger held vertically against his cheek. It may have been this, his questing eyes or his unusual, slightly sliding walk that once had prompted a bunch of scaffolding erectors to whistle after him and call down from on high: 'All right there, queen? Give us a kiss.' Monty had smiled his gratitude and gone his way feeling marvellous.

For the return home from the Retreat House, it had

132

been agreed that the Hazelhursts would bring Monty back to Hurworth late in the afternoon, by which time the Camerons would be home from Jedburgh. After drinks and some talk, Bruce would drive Jack and Bunty back to their rooms in Meadows while Estelle prepared dinner. But Monty had other ideas. Mama had left him her front door key in case an emergency arose. At his request, Jack drove him home in the morning, pausing in Meadows so that Bunty could collect her scooter, follow the car to Suicide Gardens and bring Jack back home riding pillion.

'Scamp is up to something,' said an amused Bunty, when they were once again alone. She removed her space-age crash helmet and laid it to rest on the upright piano with the chipped and yellowed keys, two of them dumb, and added: 'He's got a surprise up his sleeve.'

She was right.

'Hello!' Estelle exclaimed, seeing her car in its usual place. She looked at her watch. 'They're back early from Stanmore.'

Bruce parked his Capri behind her Cavalier and the couple entered the bungalow, expecting to be greeted by three people instead of only one.

'Home is the hunter, home from the hill, and the sailor home from the sea,' Monty called from the kitchen. He dodged out into the hall, overjoyed by the sight of astonished faces, said 'Welcome!' and dodged back in again.

'What's all this?' Estelle, slightly annoyed, asked her husband.

'Whatever it is, it smells good,' he replied.

Working non-stop for three hours, with a smile never far from his lips, Monty had prepared not only a warm and shining interior, but also a succulent dinner of chilled watercress soup, gammon with apricot stuffing and, as dessert, strawberry ice cream.

But before serving it, he propelled Bruce and Estelle

into their usual armchairs, gave them dry sherry and made them tell him, undeterred by his frequent dives into the kitchen ('Carry on! I can still hear you') every detail of their week in the Borders.

'Like on our last visit, we stayed in guest houses and set off every morning with the other riders for a day in the hills,' Bruce explained, raising his voice to be heard by his stepson and glancing self-consciously at his wife.

'Sounds splendid,' came from the kitchen. 'Pity you didn't take Cromwell and Countess. How they would have revelled in those wide open spaces! I'm sure End Point would have lent you their double box.'

'Neither of our cars has a tow-bar,' Bruce responded.

'Countess is too slow for trail riding,' Estelle said. 'You can have him now. Mrs Macdonald will buy Cromwell to ride herself. If we want to carry on hacking, we'll use school horses.'

Monty demanded, emerging afresh: 'But what about your fox-hunting?'

Estelle answered: 'I've decided not to join the Hermitage Hunt and Ibzy hasn't taken to the chase.'

'I wish I could say I was crying into my Château Latour, but I can't,' said the boy. 'To table now, the pair of you, and no nonsense. I'm ready to serve.'

Disconcerted, Cameron and Estelle looked at one another before gradually following instructions.

Monty untied his flowered apron (a birthday present from him to Mama), then joined them at a table faultlessly laid and decorated with dahlias and lilies, picked from the garden not an hour before. He poured chilled hock to accompany the delicious soup while Bruce explained that the Jedburgh stables were kept by John Tough and his wife, whose dozen or so horses were powerful and free-moving.

'You'll be old enough to come with us next year,' Estelle told Monty, 'and you'll quickly become a

Scotophile, like Ibzy and me, feasting off haggis with bashed-tatties-and-neeps and sipping single malt whisky. We'd like to live nearer, wouldn't we, Ibzy? Long, sweeping gallops through gorse and heather, some bare-back riding, and a glorious high tea at one of our night stops.'

Bruce added: 'You should have seen Mama frater-nising with two French cavalry officers who were in our party.'

'They were from Saumur. L'Ecole du Cadre Noir. And I wasn't fraternising,' Estelle pointed out, giving her husband a fond smile. 'Just conversing in French to make them feel at home.'

Answering a question, Monty said the highlight of his week with the Hazelhursts had been a visit to the Rolls-Royce Motorcar works at Crewe, where a tour of the shop floor ended among the completed cars standing in the showroom. Once again, as at Tatton Hall, his breath had been taken from him, this time not by the elegance of the setting but by the beauty and luxury of new Rolls-Royce and Bentley cars awaiting collection by their buyers.

'Faced with magnificence, one searches desperately for unused superlatives,' he informed his audience, his manner half-resigned, half-sorrowing. 'Owners choose their individual colour schemes for body and interior alike. For ours, Mama and Ibzy, I chose cream hide with polished walnut trim for the inside and jade-over-olive for what engineers rather depressingly call "the carcass". I told them you'd pay COD, Mama. Cash.'

'That was thoughtful of you,' Estelle murmured, unamused and with lowered eyes.

Bruce asked to be reminded of the name given to the flying lady radiator cap supplied by Rolls-Royce. Was it *Spirit of the Wind* or was it *Spirit of Ecstasy*?

'*Spirit of the Wind* was designed by René Lalique for

the Minerva motorcar,' Estelle said. 'Don't ask me how I know that. It's just one of those scraps of knowledge we pick up in life. Lalique was a Frenchman who created beautiful artefacts in misty glass.'

'Mama is right,' said Monty. *'Spirit of Ecstasy* adorns the Rolls-Royce. Solid silver – even gold, if you're completely mad. Can be unscrewed, notably by thieves, and replaced with a flat and somewhat tedious plug. I'll fetch the pudding.'

'Your son has suddenly grown up,' Cameron murmured, when the boy was out of the room. 'It must be the long trousers.'

His mother nodded without answering. Her silences were becoming more frequent and introspective and she was easily irritated. There was still no sign of her Dawnia, but there were distressing indications of an early start to the menopause.

At the end of the meal, Bruce said he would fetch their cases out of the car. Estelle was back in her armchair, gently massaging her brow with one hand and with the other picking at the hem of her skirt. Monty meanwhile, having forbidden her to enter the kitchen, was lustily washing up while singing along with his transistor radio.

Bruce paused, keys in hand, on his way out to the Capri, to say quietly to his wife: 'How d'you feel, my love? Is there anything I can get for you? Aspirin?'

She smiled up at him and took his hand for a moment, saying: 'I'm fine. A little tired, that's all. Not as tired as you must be though. You should have let me take a turn at driving.'

'Rest now and we'll have a drink together before kip.'

'Righty.'

She was alone, abstracted, nursing unhappiness, when startled by Monty's sudden presence beside her armchair.

He fell to his knees, pressing his palms together as if

136

in prayer, and said softly: 'Mama! Mama, I know what I want to be, Mama. A ballet dancer.'

Enraged, Estelle rounded on him, thrusting forward in her chair but remaining seated.

'You little pansy!' she shouted in his face. 'Don't dare say that again. Go to your room this minute and change back into your short pants.'

The boy fled, slammed his door behind him and threw himself down on his bed. Following almost at once, Estelle found him prostrate, sobbing into his pillow. Calm now, but distraught and not entirely repentant, she sank down at his side and began stroking his head.

'I'm sorry, Monty. Sorry for what I said. I'm not well, but that's no excuse. Forgive me, my darling.'

'I thought I'd pleased you, Mama,' Monty replied, his voice muffled by the pillow.

Estelle gently turned him onto his side and pushed hair away from his tear-wet face. They kissed with closed eyes and open lips and the boy said: 'I love you, Mama.'

'We love each other, Monty, and we'll always be together. Only death can part us and even then not for long.'

Estelle hated herself for what she had called him. He was her son. He was what she had made him. And in her heart she wanted him to stay like that.

Chapter Seven

It was not until her husband was invited to a second interview with Blanchard Brothers that Estelle showed more than polite interest in the possibility of his being appointed sales manager/director designate.

She was rather proud of him. Bruce had always maintained that he was nothing, a mere producer of dung, yet he had shown initiative in switching to a sales career when shipbuilding went into decline, tenacity in completing his marketing correspondence course, and self-confidence in applying for this new and challenging position.

Estelle said: 'I told Old Isoscelys. He responded with the Champêtre accolade – silence, then a grunt of approval. Do you know how many other candidates are standing in line?'

'There'll be at least two,' Monty said, 'in case one gets cold feet.'

'Three. Maybe four,' Bruce ventured.

The Camerons were seated in Blanchard's London showroom, waiting for Rory Baxter, European general administrator for Ditton Priors Incorporated. He was American, as were his employers, married to an English yachtswoman and living in Warwickshire, the county to which DPI had recently moved their United Kingdom headquarters from the City of London.

'They're into all sorts of enterprises, even funeral

furnishing, and diversifying all the time,' Bruce said. 'They picked off Blanchard Brothers only a year ago, and Rory told me at my first interview that their next conquest will be Tadler's paper mills.'

'It's Rory already, is it?' Estelle remarked, smiling. 'I do believe my toad is coming up to date at last.'

'His idea. Rory is an Irish name, meaning red-headed,' said Bruce.

'You look very calm, Ibzy,' Monty observed, 'but aren't you just a teensy-weensy bit nervous? I know I should be.'

'Don't talk like that, dear,' his mother said, embarrassed for him.

Bruce told her she looked lovely, adding: 'Doesn't she, Scamp?'

'Mama is never less than bewitching,' the boy lisped.

Her plain navy skirt and white tunic with blue piping at the cuffs and revers – her *costume d'appartement,* as she called the combination – had been exchanged for a pink worsted suit with amber beads and earrings and matching high-heeled shoes.

'I can't wait to admire Mama in her new cocktail dress,' Monty resumed. 'She was very naughty and refused to let me see it when she brought it home from the dressmaker's. Look over the road, the pair of you, at that Bentley pausing outside Brown's Hotel and tell me if it isn't the last word. Not my colour, red, by any manner of means, but totally must-have just the same.'

'I'll wear my dress this evening,' Estelle promised.

Monty asked her if they would be dining at Brown's. She looked at her husband, who said: 'Why not? We enjoyed our lunch there.'

The trio had reached London that morning by train from Chester, travelling first class, and had taken a taxi to Brown's Hotel, where they were occupying a suite paid for by Estelle as Bruce's birthday present.

'Can I get you a drink while you're waiting?' the showroom manager asked from his desk at the other end of the room. 'Tea? Coffee? Something stronger perhaps? I have an excellent month-old port. Rory is evidently held up somewhere.'

'He's crossing the road now,' Cameron answered, watching him through the window and noticing afresh his sprightly walk, the head a little forward, as if he couldn't wait to get there. 'When I was here last, it took me an age to find a parking place. Remember, Monty?'

'Check.'

'Rory's had the same problem, I suppose,' Bruce added.

He rose with his stepson when Baxter came through the door, and introduced Estelle, who remained seated, one long thigh crossed over the other.

'I remember Monty,' Rory said, smiling and nodding and vigorously shaking hands all round. 'Follow me upstairs and I'll show you the apartment. Sorry I'm late. Today has been one of those days.'

He would be unable to spend the rest of the afternoon with the Camerons, driving them out to the Cricklewood factory as planned, but would they join him for dinner at the Café Royal that evening?

They would.

Leading the way up to the flat, Rory added: 'We can talk there in peace and I can answer any queries you may have about the job, Bruce. Now this is the living room and it overlooks Albemarle Street.'

'There's Brown's, Mama,' Monty, already at the window, announced approvingly.

'Our present sales manager is moving out at the end of the month,' Rory explained. 'He has lived here alone since his wife died. Over the years, he's been buying a house for his retirement and letting tenants pay the mortgage for him. A wise economist. A sharp salesman too. We're sorry he's going.'

'Is the furniture going with him?' Estelle asked, eyeing it coldly.

Like the furniture at home, it was adequate but uninspiring. Bruce was still surprised and a little disappointed that Estelle had changed nothing at Hurworth.

'A dealer has bought it,' Rory replied, moving forward now to the two bedrooms.

He had to duck to pass through doorways. Tall and lean, with a small head, he had the longest feet Monty had ever seen. Viewed from the side, he reminded the boy of a forklift truck in the rest position.

Clicking a light on and then off as he spoke, Rory continued: 'Once the apartment is empty, Blanchard's will pay for new decorations, which it will be for you or whoever gets the job to choose. The kitchen and bathroom are all that's left to see. Then, regrettably, we'll have to part company till this evening.'

He began it at seven o'clock with cocktails and a neatly-turned compliment for Estelle, radiant in her off-the-shoulder dress of bronze satin, exquisitely fashioned and worn with silk stockings the colour of brandy and fragile evening shoes. Her pearls and diamonds Bruce was seeing for the first time, since they normally resided in the strong room at Barclay's Bank in Chester.

'I thought everyone in London wore evening dress, Ibzy, in a setting like this,' Monty said, plainly crestfallen at the absence of white tie and tails.

'Not these days. Formal attire didn't come back after the Second World War,' Bruce told him. To Rory, he explained: 'My stepson is an admirer of Roy Fox, an American gentleman who led a dance band over here in the nineteen thirties and was famous for looking as if he'd been poured into his evening clothes.'

'Society dance music. Little tunes played prettily,'

Rory responded, tolerantly. 'I'm a Wagner addict myself. Mighty, mighty Wagner! What about you, Estelle?'

'Oh, a little of most things, from Beethoven to the Beatles,' she answered. 'I'm not crazy about music, I have to confess, or literature. I get on with my knitting and my gardening and leave the finer things in life to my son and my husband.'

'She flatters me,' said Bruce. 'The Rolling Stones and Anthony Quinnis are the extent of my cultural interests.'

Over dinner in the many-mirrored restaurant, whose red plush and gilded chairs had long before caused Max Beerbohm, at first sight of them, to exclaim 'This is life!', Rory Baxter, prompted by Estelle's slight accent, asked what part of the United States she was from. Boston?

Smiling, she replied: 'Quebec.'

Monty said: 'We're pea-soupers, Mama and me. Ibzy's a limey.'

Rory knew what a limey was, but not a pea-souper.

'It's what Canadians call French Canadians when they wish to be hurtful,' Estelle explained.

'Well well indeed! So you and your son are French speakers,' Baxter suggested.

'It's our first language,' said Estelle. 'We speak only French at home.'

'Bruce too?'

'My husband is competent in all four branches of French – speaking, understanding, reading and writing.'

Estelle fingered soft brown hair away from one eye, tilted her head slightly and smiled at Cameron. He covered her hand with his and said: 'What I've achieved, Rory, is thanks entirely to my schoolmistress here. Estelle is as strict as she's beautiful and I love her for both those things.'

At Hurworth every Sunday evening, in the room they

142

called the office, teacher and pupil spent an hour or more together, Estelle sitting at the desk, Bruce seated at her side. She gave him dictation, marked the work he had done in hotel rooms, and set fresh exercises for the week to come. While she corrected his few mistakes, some of them made deliberately, his attention would stray to the thick ebony ruler close to her right hand and from it to the accommodating thighs inside the knee-length navy skirt and he would envy the boy they could hear playing his practice pieces beyond the closed door. These were among Cameron's happiest moments, flawed only by the longing he still could not bring himself to express.

'You like making me work hard, don't you?' he would murmur between kisses, when they were naked together in bed. 'You won't let me get away with so much as a misplaced comma, will you?'

Those favourite words of his, those verbs of compulsion and constraint, backed by the vision of chastisement at the hands of his wife, enhanced his carnal thrust, pleasing her yet making her wonder why, with his fertility no longer in doubt, she did not conceive. Irregular intervals between periods were continually raising and dashing her hopes, resulting in mood changes that made her difficult to live with, especially for Monty, who was there all the time and to whom she could not explain and justify the reason.

True to her social class, she avoided burdening other people with her misfortunes. 'Who'd be a woman?' was as far as she went, and then only with Bunty Hazelhurst, who could empathise because she was already enduring the sweating, the headaches and the weight-gain that awaited Estelle.

She asked Rory Baxter if he and his wife had children.

'Three. Three girls. One of them is reading law at Oxford, another wants to be a medical doctor, and number three can't decide whether she wants to be a nurse or an architect.'

Estelle said, smiling at her son and in a voice that left no room for argument: 'Monty is going to be a doctor of music. He takes his Grade One examination next week, which is the first rung on a long ladder. Then he can have a few days' travelling with Bruce before starting to prepare for Grade Two. '

'What if I don't pass Grade One, Mama?' Monty teased.

Laughing, he threw up his hands to protect his face.

'Think positively,' Estelle retorted. 'Don't ever succumb to the English vice of negative thinking. You're a Canadian, a French Canadian, and I want you always to remain so, because we belong to a young nation that hasn't lost its vitality, its optimism and its pioneering spirit. We're not jaded.'

'Like me,' said Bruce, squirting lemon juice onto his Dover sole.

'Like the Brits in general and the English in particular,' his wife maintained. 'You've had it so good for so long that you're like spoilt children. Your Welfare State, admirable though it is, has taken the challenge out of life. It has drawn your teeth.'

Cameron asked: 'Is that true, Monty? Do different nationalities show different characteristics? Come on! You're a literate and observant young man.'

'Oh, I think it's self-evident,' the boy replied, in his rapid-fire and confident way. 'Climate, history, language, must all shape character. Add to that education, social mores and prosperity or the lack of it and you have your answer.'

'What do you think of the Brits, Rory?' Bruce asked. 'Tell the truth.'

Baxter was lost in contemplation of Monty, whose feminine beauty and staccato delivery raised questions in

144

his mind. He came back to the subject as if from a daydream to say that he shared Estelle's opinion.

'When I look at your country, Bruce, I see old age. A nation that for two hundred years led the world in enterprise and innovation is happy now to watch television and leave someone else to do the thinking.'

'Every great nation has its hour at the feast,' Monty responded crisply. He took a sip from his second glass of wine, which Estelle had told him was his limit. 'Consider Egypt under the pharaohs, Rome under the caesars, Persia under Darius, Macedonia under Philip and later his brilliant son, Alexander. Their star rose, traversed the heavens, and fell to earth. Now it's North America's turn.'

'And after us, who?' asked Rory Baxter. 'China, India, Saudi Arabia? The initiative will return to the East, from whence it came, because they will have the energy in both meanings of the word, and the West will gradually become their vassal. Yesterday, I heard one of your senior politicians advocating Britain's withdrawal from the European Union. That would be a very foolish move. Should Big Brother arise to dominate Europe, he will be in Brussels and he might be tempted to invade and subjugate an independent Britain.'

'Whatever else they've lost, the Brits haven't lost their good manners,' Estelle told Baxter. 'They're not as shut-in as the French, who often look as though they're nursing small grievances, or as arrogant as the Germans. I've witnessed French as well as German behaviour in Chester, where we get a lot of them in summer, and now in London.'

Monty said: 'I should think all nationalities get a bit above themselves when they're abroad and in a group, the more so if they are very-nicely-thank-you, as one tends to be on vacation.'

Still tickled and intrigued, smiling Baxter gave Monty

a long, steady look containing an element of puzzlement. To divert his attention, Estelle started describing an entry she had come across in the *Oxford Dictionary of Music* in Gorman Public Library. 'It seems that here in Britain, by a custom dating back to the thirteenth century, the Archbishop of Canterbury is empowered to grant academic degrees. His Grace has been known, when in a benign mood, to exercise this prerogative by conferring the doctorate of music.'

Contentedly, Monty remarked: 'Spoken like the dictionary itself, Mama.'

'His Grace!' Bruce snorted. 'How ridiculous can we get? Your Eminence. My Lord. How much longer are we going to tolerate these fatuous and outmoded titles? Their Majesties. Your Excellency.'

'You have a lot of them in Britain, some quite charming,' Estelle mused, 'though not to a gentleman I know in Quebec. Papa goes off like a hand grenade at the mere mention of them. He has never forgiven a friend of his for accepting the Order of Canada. A man is what he achieves, he likes to say, and achievement is the only valid distinction.'

'Titles and decorations are fit only for royalty and played-out politicians,' Bruce declared. He turned to Baxter with: 'In this country, Rory, we have the House of Commons and the House of Lords, the latter being tangible proof of life after death, as a trade union leader, Jack Jones by name, once famously said. Before reaching senility – sometimes only just before – senior Commoners can expect to receive honours and a seat in the Lords. This is a demonstration of parliamentarians seeing each other right regardless of party, convictions or no convictions at all. A glance at the majority of them, incidentally, makes me aware of how few people want to be in Parliament.'

Studying her with admiring eyes, Baxter said: 'I think

Estelle wants to tell us something more about the Archbishop of Canterbury.'

'He has piles,' said Monty.

His mother flashed him a look that scorched his bottom.

'He issues his degrees from his London palace,' she said, 'and they are called Lambeth or sometimes Canterbury degrees.'

'But would he grant one to a Roman Catholic?' Bruce wondered aloud. 'I'm looking at Monty Cameron.'

Estelle saw no reason why he should not. 'After all, the custom was established before the Reformation, when Britain was a Roman Catholic country and the Archbishop of Canterbury was appointed by the Pope.'

Monty said: 'Maybe he'll throw me one for old times' sake, or maybe Old Isoscelys will call him to say I belong to the distinguished House of Champêtre and what's the big idea refusing me?'

'I should mention, Mr Baxter, that Old Isoscelys is my son's disrespectful name for my father,' Estelle said, showing her amusement.

'If your father is Louis de Champêtre, I once played golf with him,' Rory said.

'Never! I hope you let him win,' Estelle responded.

'I truly can't remember who bought the beer. It's a few years ago now. There were four of us and I was young and outclassed. Nowadays I'm just outclassed.'

'A foursome at golf or bridge is called a *quatuor* in Quebec,' said Estelle. 'Papa's golfing days are done, I'm afraid. Like my poor mother, he can hardly leave his chair without a helping hand from *le petit personnel*. We got a call last night, didn't we, Bruce, to say his sister, Aunt Didi, had passed away in her sleep? He was very broken up over it. *"C'est le commencement de la fin"* he said.'

'Are you going to Canada for the funeral?' Cameron asked. 'Have you made up your mind?'

147

'I think the three of us should spend a week or two at *Les Merles,* but not until Scamp's exam is out of the way,' said Estelle.

Monty was rubbing his hands.

'Besides,' his mother told Bruce, 'Bunty needs our support at the moment.'

'*Your* support,' he corrected.

'Very well – mine. Jack is in bed and often in cruel pain. The man I am speaking of, Mr Baxter, is dying of cancer, *le fléau du siècle.* Strangely, the only way he can find relief is by lying on his side.'

Bruce said he would buy Jack a bottle of Lochan Ora before leaving London. 'It's a superb liqueur whisky. Expensive, but worth every penny.'

Impishly, Monty asked Estelle if she was going to tell Rory Baxter what Jack had said when Father Coglan came over from St Mary's to pay him a visit.

'No I am not,' she answered, decisively, 'and neither are you.'

'Ah, go on! Let me, Mama. Let me.'

'I'm longing to hear this,' Rory said, glancing up from signing for the dinner.

'Oh, very well,' Estelle conceded. 'I don't suppose it spells the end of Christendom.'

Beside himself with glee, Monty said: 'Bunty went into the sickroom and announced to Jack that the priest was downstairs. Jack pulled the bedclothes over his head and growled *"Tell him to go to hell. I'll see him there".*'

2

The boy knew ahead of the results that he had failed his Grade One. As he explained to Bruce when they were travelling together, he had known while sitting his GCSE examinations in French, English, history and mathematics that he was going to pass because Estelle had prepared him properly.

Bunty had not.

'I didn't know the half of what was expected of me,' he said, in a voice hoarse with sadness and disappointment.

'Have you told Mama?' Bruce asked.

Monty shook his head and stared through the windscreen. They were sitting in the Capri, parked in a layby near Coventry. Bruce had just switched off the radio after listening with his stepson to *The World at One* on BBC Radio 4 while eating salmon sandwiches and sipping orange juice.

'There's just a chance I've passed, Ibzy. I don't know how high their standards are. But if I have, it will be conclusive evidence that I'm a living marvel.'

'What have you said to Bunty?'

'Nothing. I don't want to cause distress.'

'But, Monty, she led Mama to believe you'd sail through it. So Mama is going to blame you, not Bunty, if you fail.'

'Let's just wait and see, Ibzy. Mama isn't herself right now and Bunting is at her wits' end over Jack. When I called home last night, Mama said he'd gone into hospital.'

Estelle never asked to speak with her husband during these nightly telephone conversations, and Cameron found sexual pleasure in his exclusion, just as he did in referring to Estelle as Mama. He told himself that his wife could treat him as she wished: that he was hers to exclude or ignore, praise or punish, exactly as if he were Monty all over again.

The boy said: 'I'm worried about Mama.'

'You and me both, Monty, which is why I've asked you to lay off teasing her about becoming a ballet dancer. She thinks you mean it and it's flustering her.'

149

'I do mean it.'

'Be patient, Monty. You're sixteen. Time is on your side.'

'Wrong, Ibzy. Those who get to the top are those who start early. You've said that yourself.'

'I'll talk to her.'

'Oh, would you?'

But Cameron knew that Estelle would refuse to listen. He had never seen her so upset as when her son pleaded for a career on the stage instead of the concert platform. 'Stop that talk at once,' she snapped, 'before I lose my temper.' Sophisticated though she was in manners, dress and behaviour, Estelle had little experience of life outside the schoolroom. It was her belief that all male ballet dancers were homosexual and her Faith condemned homosexuality as among the worst of sins.

'Which it is not,' Bruce told Monty, wishing to put the boy at ease with his sexual orientation. 'Unnatural, okay, undesirable even, but in no way sinful if confined to consenting adults. Like four-letter words, sex in all its forms should be pulled out into the open. Sex is clean and joyful, Monty, never sinful and never dirty. This notion of dirtiness may be due to its being kept in the dark for so long, like rats under floor boards, or to the nearness of our genitals to our sewage outlets. Bookworm that you are, you will have heard of W.B. Yeats. He made the point better than I can when he wrote *"Love pitched its tent in the place of excrement"*. But that is the only sense in which sex can be regarded as dirty, so rid your mind of it.'

'You're not Catholic, Ibzy.'

'No. Catholics and all within the Anglican communion belong to the Church of Christ Scapegoat. Like Jack Hazelhurst, I'm a Nazarene, a follower to the best of my ability of the true Jesus and a founder member of the Church of Christ Humanist. We believe that the Old

150

Testament, with its blood and thunder, is life as we know it, whilst the New, with its sweetness and light, is life as it ought to be. That said, of course, the Ten Commandments are in the Old and they are all anyone needs by way of a religion. If children of all Faiths and denominations were required to recite them every morning at Assembly, our world would be a better place. Was your father a Catholic by birth, Monty, or did he change for Mama? She told me once, but I've forgotten.'

'He changed.'

'Did Mama make him?' Bruce asked, wanting to hear that she had.

'I don't know.'

'But she dominated CB, didn't she? You say she beat him sometimes.'

The boy nodded. Cameron asked why she beat him. 'What did he do to make her want to abuse him?'

'It was always the sawmill. He had to bring the books home and if he'd had a poor month he was for it. Once she used her cutting whip on him. It was horrible.'

'How did Clyde react? Did he never fight back?'

'He just used to flatten himself against the wall and say *"There's no need for this, Estelle"*. Mama would shout at him and tell him to think of ways of improving business, to get out of his nice warm office and into his car and go *find* orders.'

'To please Old Isoscelys.'

'Mama was the one he had to please,' Monty corrected, quietly.

He went on to say that, the beatings aside, his mother and father had lived together peaceably. Estelle liked to watch television while knitting, but she didn't object if Clyde wanted the set switched off so that he could read the evening paper or the book he had borrowed from Gorman Public Library. Their likes and dislikes had been similar, except that Clyde enjoyed watching football and

151

occasionally going with Jack to see a match. Once in a while they had played cards with him and Bunty, either at the Hazelhursts' rooms opposite St Mary's Church in Meadows or at the Beaumonts' apartment in what Monty continued to call Oildrum Court.

Wishing to renew his secret enjoyment, Cameron asked if Mama had ever humiliated Clyde.

'How d'you mean?'

'I was just wondering if she ever put him over her knee,' Bruce said, pretending amusement while savouring the words.

She hadn't.

A pause. Then smiling Monty admitted: 'That pleasure was reserved for me.'

'Was?'

'Yes. Times have changed, Ibzy, and now I'm faced with the bleak prospect of growing up.'

The morning lessons had ended following excellent GCSE results and Mama no longer spanked him even when he teased or wilfully disobeyed her. He must now be reasoned with. Long trousers had become his everyday dress and Estelle was making him a weekly allowance to spend as he chose. Her boy was on the threshold of man's estate and a distinguished career at the keyboard.

Lighting his pipe and running the window down on his side of the car, Bruce said: 'A woman's life is harder than a man's, Monty. They get the dirty end of most sticks, not least the reproductive one. You'll know what I mean later on, if the End Point girls haven't already opened your eyes.'

'I don't think they've left much for me to discover, Ibzy.'

'Be nice to Mama. Clown around, the way you did on Sunday, when you had both of us laughing.'

After dinner, standing on the hearthrug with his back

to the sitting room fire, Monty had recited his latest limericks ('Careful!' Mama had cautioned at one point), had sung comic songs, repeated jokes heard at the riding centre and gone through his parody of a call centre:

'Welcome to the Emergency Services.

If your house is on fire, press One now.

If you're being raped, press Two.

If you're being bludgeoned to death, press Three.

Thank you for making your selection. Your call will be dealt with as soon as our advisers return from lunch.'

For his finale, Monty, with raised right arm, stick-on moustache and raucous voice had mimicked Hitler while wearing on his head one of Bruce's enamel pudding basins. His encore was his party piece. Crossing his eyes, he wiggled his ears without moving the rest of his face, causing Estelle to warn him that he could stick like that.

She still hadn't sought confirmation from her doctor, but increasingly depressing signs were enough to tell her that her Monty would never have a sibling. Bunty could testify that her friend faced two years or more of hot flushes, sweating and dizzy spells. A perfectionist in all she did, Estelle was maddened by compromise, by impediments to the routine of everyday life. She found herself waking in the night, seized by panic fear or drained by suicidal hopelessness. When Bunty asked if she had considered adopting or fostering, her answer was: 'No woman wants another woman's child.'

Although she was hiding her unhappiness from Bruce, he detected it and did what he could to comfort her. 'I'm better when you're here,' she would say, when they were sitting together on the sofa and holding hands. Monty too, older than his years, knew when and how to be tender; but for all his feminine sensitivity, he was unable to offer the warmth and understanding which, Estelle believed, would be in the gift of a daughter.

153

She was her bright and positive self by the time her husband and son returned home from four nights at the Regent Hotel in Leamington Spa and the better part of five days' selling in the Midlands, 'now vastly enriched by numerous pots and pans, to say nothing of an air rifle and two Tilley lamps' Monty told her over dinner, adding, with kindness slowing his normally rapid speech: 'Forgive me, Ibzy, if I have my little joke.'

Bruce chided him for slipping into the Englishman's flippant attitude to selling. 'I wish you had heard Rory Baxter's views on the subject. He said that in the States, selling is classed as a profession, highly respected and handsomely rewarded.'

'As it is in Canada,' Estelle responded. 'Papa has always sent me a copy of the minutes of Board meetings, but now, more and more, he's including copies of other business matters and you should see the kind of money our top salesmen are earning. Over here, I gather, selling is held in low esteem. Bunty told me once about a neighbour of hers, a man, who was given a job as a rep after his position as a production manager ceased to exist. 'It'll do while he looks for something better' his wife said to Bunty, as though selling is for those of us who are fit for nothing else.'

'Most people reduce it to the same level as writing novels or being a Member of Parliament. Writer and talker alike should get a proper job,' said Bruce. 'The salesman in Britain, even in senior management, still bears the stigma of the fast-talking, foot-in-the-door hustler with an eye for the bored housewife and a fund of dirty jokes. Also – and this baffles me – there is a widespread belief that earning commission is somehow shameful. I'm reminded of the class-ridden British Army of days gone by, when internal communications were sometimes addressed to "officers and their ladies, NCOs and their wives, private soldiers and their women". The

154

similarity is that fees are honourable and salaries respectable, but *commission!* There's something contemptible, even slimy, about it, like accepting backhanders.'

'We stole a peek at the Ditton Priors headquarters while we were touring in Warwickshire, didn't we, Ibzy?' Monty revealed. 'An impressive building. High, wide and handsome. Looking almost pink in the setting sun.'

'Ditton Priors. Who are they?' his mother asked, without interest.

Slightly hurt, Bruce countered with: 'You've forgotten? They own Blanchard Brothers.'

'Also Landslide Developments, Sunstroke Holidays, Moonshine Investments and Complete Fabrications Limited,' added Monty.

'When d'you expect to hear if you've got the London job?' Estelle asked.

'Rory Baxter said by the end of this month.'

'Roaring Baxter,' Monty declared, bouncing in his seat. 'Five times married and always to the same woman. I call that devotion.'

'Have less to say, please,' his mother warned him. 'What else did you do, Bruce, when you weren't selling hardware?'

'We sneaked an afternoon off, Scamp and I, to watch sheepdog trials. We heard the story of an English sheep farmer who bought a collie from a farmer in Wales, but had to return it because it only understood orders called out in Welsh.'

Estelle had asked her husband to try to interest Monty in 'manly things', so he had taken the boy to a game fair and for a ride on the Severn Valley Railway from Bridgnorth to Kidderminster and back. Cameron's love affair with steam traction, be it on road or rail, dated back to his schooldays, when he and his friend bought

155

platform tickets and spent Saturday mornings watching trains enter and leave Liverpool Lime Street. He loved the smell given off by an engine in-steam – a delicious blend of warm oil, hot steel and coal smoke. But Monty, whilst having enjoyed the leisurely ride through captivating scenery, dismissed the locomotive that had hauled their train as 'rather a dirty beast, Ibzy. Let's go into the gift shop and see if we can find a little something to take home to Mama, like an old railway sleeper.'

The highlight of the boy's week had been *Macbeth* at Stratford until eclipsed by a matinée performance of *La Bayadère* by the Royal Ballet Company in Birmingham. Bruce spent the afternoon in the nearby Science & Industry Museum, where he was joined towards closing time by a stepson still intoxicated by what he had seen, especially the *Kingdom of Shades* sequence, choreographed by Nureyev.

'Don't let Mama know you went there,' Bruce warned him at the time. 'Keep that between ourselves.'

'Check.'

'You came with me to the museum, where we gazed open-mouthed at the magnificent steam loco called *City of Birmingham*. Got it? If Mama discovered our secret, she might give each of us a good whipping. And we don't want that, Scamp, do we?'

Monty avoided a mild rebuke by telling Estelle that the present he handed her after dinner was 'from both of us, darling – Ibzy and me. I ought really to have told you to hide your eyes, but you might not have been able to find them again. We spotted it in the window of a bric-à-brac shop in Kenilworth, agreed it was must-have and spent our pennies without more ado.'

'It's beautiful,' Estelle murmured, caressing it with her small, slim hands. 'A trinket box. I wonder who its first owner was.'

The box was made of thin wood, the base covered with

red artfelt, the sides and top clad with pink mirror-glass, plain all round except for a sunray design incised on the lid.

'Nineteen thirties. Art deco,' Bruce explained.

Although he and Monty had found nothing suitable for Mama in the railway gift shop, the boy had come away with a handsome book devoted to British royal trains. A present from Bruce, it was replete with colour plates of elegant carriages and opulent interiors.

Estelle, idly turning the pages, called to her son, who was drying dishes with the kitchen door open: 'Your grandfather would disown you, young fellow, if I told him you admire the Monarchy. Isn't that so, my toad?'

'The admirer will turn into a supporter once he starts paying taxes,' Bruce replied, filling his pipe, 'and that may make him change his tune. Our Royal Family, Estelle, lives off the fat of the land without putting its hand in its pocket. Its members, plus numerous hangers-on, toil not, neither do they spin.'

'Then why do you tolerate them?' his puzzled wife wanted to know. 'They've served no useful purpose since the Restoration. To my Canadian eyes, it's simply not enough to go round grinning, launching ships and opening public conveniences.'

'I declare these lavatories open,' Monty announced from the kitchen. 'May God bless them and all who find relief in them.'

'We tolerate them because most of us don't think,' said Bruce. 'If we did, we would outlaw the crucifix as a gruesome obscenity. We would recoil in horror from a butcher's shop red with blood and a delivery van hung with corpses. But familiarity has bred indifference – to everything from the unforgivable cruelty of keeping a bird in a cage to the lavish lifestyle of a family that has its private railway train, its fleet of limousines, its string of racehorses, its priceless collection of art treasures, its vast personal wealth – not to mention its flight of aircraft and half-dozen palatial residences guarded by its own police force.'

'I shall visit and enjoy each and every one of them if we move south,' Monty called, over the hiss of running water. 'I'll take Mama along and make a convert of her.'

Estelle called back: 'Mama does not approve of idlers who live in luxury provided by others. Mama does not approve of greed, extravagance or callous indifference to the plight of those in need – sometimes desperate need – all over the world. She does not approve of splendid uniforms blazoned with unearned medal ribbons, of royalty's undisputed right of precedence at official and social gatherings, of the absurd convention that says the Monarch may not be touched or directly addressed by letter. Like Ibzy, Mama condemns the demeaning practice of addressing another mere mortal as Your Royal Highness. Such rot has no place in today's world outside of musical comedy.'

'Spoken like a Quaker,' Bruce said, in approval and admiration. 'I never suspected that such passion smouldered behind your cool demeanour.'

'I don't want him to become anglicised,' murmured Estelle. Then, raising her voice, she forced home once again that she and her son were not British. 'We are French Canadians and always will be, even if we spend the rest of our lives outside Canada.'

The boy came to the kitchen doorway, where, in Estelle's flowered apron and rubber gloves, he stood smiling benignly upon his mother and stepfather.

'Honestly!' he protested, with exaggerated outrage. 'There's not a grain of romance to split between the pair of you. What does it take to cheat thee of a sigh or charm thee to a tear? Have you no feeling for tradition, grace, elegance, pageantry? Darlings, you're so fearfully suburban, so shamelessly materialistic. Look beyond timber and Tilley lamps for just one moment and behold the visual feast that is the British Royal Family.'

Estelle looked over at her husband, her face taut with disapprobation.

Monty concluded: 'Mama doesn't live in regal splendour, but neither does she earn her own living. Her money is provided by others. And as for you, noble Ibzy, enemy of blood sports, what on earth are you doing applying for a job with a manufacturer of shotguns?'

'I think you've made your point,' said Estelle, coldly, on her way to answer the telephone.

It was Bunty.

3

Cameron believed that Earth is a penal settlement to which we are sent as punishment for sins committed elsewhere. This explained for him the varying length of our sentences, the varying degree of our suffering, and the otherwise meaningless aphorism 'Whom the gods love die young'. Also, it justified the existence of evil: cruel and mean-spirited people are here to punish us. We are sent to Earth from a better place and it is possible that we return to it at the end of a sentence that could be as short as an hour or as long as a century. Magic exists there. Children start their sentence believing in it and do not altogether lose that belief until they are seven – called by some the Age of Reason, by romantics the Age of Disillusionment. Throughout our lives, we experience rare and tantalising moments when we glimpse magic, only to see it melt away as we try to prolong it.

Jack Hazelhurst, unable to reconcile Auschwitz with Bunty's belief in an all-knowing, all-powerful God, died an atheist. He had held no theories about where we come from or where we go afterwards. He had shown no respect for life, which he considered a burden, and none for death, which he had called extinction. More wickedness, he used to say, has been perpetrated in the name of God than in any other name. As for the world's religions, they have never united men: they have always set them against each other. He excluded women because they do not foregather, throw up leaders and foment trouble. Women create life: men destroy it.

Having nothing to leave save a collection of dated and extensively mended clothes, Jack had not made a Will. He told Bunty that his body, being toxic waste, should be burnt without ceremony and with the minimum of delay. His last wish, he said, was that the furnaceman, as he slammed the oven door, should shout 'Be gone, oaf! Enough of you'. He wanted his ashes thrown into the dustbin. 'Only a ghoul keeps them on the mantelpiece.'

Saying nothing of this to anyone, Bunty asked God to forgive her for disregarding Jack's wish to be cremated. Instead, she had him buried in St Mary's churchyard, in a grave she could see from their bedroom, a grave in which, when her time came, she would be reunited with him.

She deeply regretted that he had gone through life without 'finding Jesus', belief in whose divine will had always sustained her, making tolerable the emotionally deprived years between the loss of Leon and her union with Jack. She had never found out why Leon had gradually stopped seeing her, never discovered that her crippled mother, who wanted the railway porter, Jimmy Devine, for her son-in-law, had taken Leon aside and whispered to him that Bunty was epileptic. 'She has them fits an' all. Know what I mean? She screams an' all her mouth foams. Not a word to no one, mind! It's a family secret is that.'

160

'Mother died from peritonitis after she accidentally swallowed the sharp end of one of them plastic toothpicks,' Bunty told Estelle. 'Poor soul! She wasn't very nice to me, considering all I done for her, but she was still my mother.'

After her death, the mining company had allowed Bunty to continue living in the two-up-and-two-down until the local priest, whose housemaid she was, found her a live-in job at a girls' boarding school in Cheshire. He was retiring and going to live with his widowed sister in Scotland.

The railway porter had asked Bunty to marry him. To Estelle, she said: 'Not on your life! I went to the pictures with him once and quite frankly he had me stripped to my ankle socks before the lights went down.'

She hadn't liked the Cheshire job. Before a year was out, she had become a postwoman, bought herself a motor scooter and rented the two furnished rooms in the Bushells' house in Meadows. She was soon the admiring friend of Father Coglan, the pianist at his services and his assistant at the laying-on of hands, the ritual that had brought Jack Hazelhurst into her life.

Estelle insisted on covering the funeral expenses and she gave Bunty the one hundred pounds that she had intended giving her later on as a bonus for getting Monty through his Grade One keyboard examination. His results were still awaited, as were those of Bruce's interviews with Blanchard Brothers. Meanwhile, Estelle had started making inquiries about getting her son into the Royal College of Music in London, or, alternatively, the Royal Northern College of Music in Manchester.

'Which one I send him to will depend on Ibzy's getting or not getting this new job,' she said to Bunty. 'Also, there's the question of where we live. Do we move as a family into the London apartment that comes with the job or does Ibzy live there on his own all week and come home here at weekends? He says I'm the boss, which is news to me, so it's for me to decide.'

'And where would you prefer to live, Scamp?' Bunty asked, smiling at him. 'Hurworth or Babylon?'

'I'm doing so well with my stable management, to say nothing of my dressage, that my choice has to be Hurworth, at any rate for the time being. London later perhaps. Mrs Macdonald says I should start preparing for the Horse Owner's Certificate of the British Horse Society.'

'Tell Mrs Macdonald you're not preparing for anything except a career in music, either as a teacher or a performer, I don't care which,' Estelle informed him. Then, to Bunty: 'Since he got back from his week's vacation with Bruce, I've kept him at his daily practice, so as not to undo the good work you've done on him. I know how quickly a student can lose his facility. Learning is hard: forgetting is horribly easy.'

Added to Bunty's misery at the loss of her chap was her belief that Monty had almost certainly failed his Grade One. If so, she would go on her knees to beg the forgiveness of the woman whose faith in her teaching ability had been misplaced from the outset and whose kindness and generosity she considered overwhelming.

'Bunty supported me when I lost Clyde,' Estelle reminded Bruce. 'Now it's my turn to support her.'

Until starting a new life at Stanmore Abbey, Bunty lunched with Estelle and Monty from Monday to Friday, going home in the afternoon or serving in St Mary's charity shop, then returning to Hurworth for most of the evening. When not at End Point or walking Fiver, Monty sat round the fire with the women, chatting on equal terms and joining his mother in trying to take Bunty's mind off her bereavement. But, not sharing Estelle's contention that grief should be borne in private, never paraded nor made the cause of discomfiture in others, she kept returning to her loss, usually in tears.

162

'Poor dear! At least he went the way he hoped he'd go – in a warm bed and in full knowledge of what was happening,' she said, crying softly into a wet ball of handkerchief. 'He used to say if ever he couldn't feed himself and keep himself clean, he'd put an end to his life. *"I'm not rotting to death in a care home"*, he would say, *"or staggering along between two sticks, or humming round in an electric chair. If that comes, Cock, it'll be time to say goodbye".*'

Bunty and Estelle were both at a turning point in their lives. Estelle had to accept that the longed-for second child would never come, Bunty that the great love of her life had gone and could never be replaced.

'Think of the happy times you had together, Bunty,' Estelle urged, pausing in her knitting to pluck at the hem of her knee-length skirt. 'You had Jack to thank for the comfort a man brings to a woman, and he had you to thank for taking him in and giving him a proper home. You've never said, but I think you'd have liked children.'

'Very much, Estelle.'

Bunty would have loved a family, with her own house, her chap coming in from work and golden-haired children running along the hall to welcome him. A recurring vision was of her living room on Christmas Day, with a roaring fire, fairy lights in the tree, opened presents on the hearth rug and everyone seated round the table, paper-hatted and pulling crackers, their merriment sustained by a dinner of roast turkey and plum pudding. It would remain a daydream, like the earlier one of herself as Senga Flanagan, tall and slender, a fashion model for the House of Desmond Denise, a member of the international jet set, with Hollywood stars among her friends and a lush apartment in Manhattan.

This time it was Monty who brought her back to the homely realities of Suicide Gardens with the comment

163

that she would be as snug as the lead in a pencil once installed in the Retreat House at Stanmore Abbey.

Estelle added: 'No more getting out of bed at three in the morning, delivering letters in all weathers and going back to that cold sitting room of yours.'

'I never took you up to our bedroom,' Bunty muttered. 'Quite frankly, it's like a cold storage. Jack used to say someone had died there and was haunting it. Hot water bottles and an old paraffin stove made it bearable at bedtime, but by morning we were back to zero.'

The Abbess at Stanmore had responded to Bunty's inquiry with the offer of a post as assistant to the Guest Mistress, answering the telephone, allotting rooms to retreatants and helping in the kitchen.

'I'll have my own room and the blessing of central heating,' she said. 'It's a gift from God, just as my Jack was a gift from God. Oh, here's Brian. I was forgetting today's Friday.'

'Ibzy's early,' Monty observed.

'And my scooter's in his way,' Bunty announced, rising as she looked through the window. 'Look! He's having to leave his car in the road. I'll see you both on Monday.'

'You don't have to go because Bruce is here,' Estelle protested. 'Stay and I'll make some coffee.'

'He wants his home to himself after a week away,' said Bunty. 'That's only to be expected.'

She and Cameron crossed in the hall, eyes down and exchanging only the briefest of greetings. Then, as Monty closed the front door, Bruce took his wife in his arms, kissed her and asked if there was any news.

'Not so far, my toad,' she answered. 'It's my guess they'll arrive together – Scamp's letter and yours.'

She was right.

Next morning, returning alone from the car wash, Cameron found The Terrible Trio standing watching the bungalow in awed silence. Absently, they moved aside to let his car through onto the drive. When he stepped out of it, the reason for their mute fascination became audible.

Monty was howling. Thinking he had had an accident, Bruce made quickly for the kitchen. The boy was bent over the table, both hands gripping the edge furthest from him. His trousers were round his ankles, his underpants round his knees, his shirt tail flicked clear of his bottom. Estelle, enraged, was caning him with swift, biting strokes. A letter and its envelope lay at her feet.

'You deliberately failed, didn't you?' she was shouting. 'You little demon. That way you thought I'd let you switch to ballet. Well, this is the only switching you get – this and plenty more of it.'

Such was her concentrated fury and Monty's yelling that she remained unaware of her husband's approach until he snatched the cane out of her raised hand.

She spun round.

'Give me that cane. Don't you dare interfere. Give it back to me this minute.'

Gripping it by its ends, Cameron bent the cane into an arc. It shattered. He tossed it aside and said: 'You're not flogging him, Estelle.'

'I'll do as I please,' she retorted, fists on hips. 'He's my son, not yours.'

Coughing, choking, pulling up his trousers, Monty scuttled into a corner as Bruce repeated, slowly and firmly: 'You are not flogging him, Estelle. Spanking, okay, but beating with a cane is out. Go to your room, Monty.'

The boy didn't move. Crouching, shivering, he stayed with his face to the wall, clutching his buttocks and crying quietly. The blossoming adult of recent days, fluent and over-confident, was a child again.

'He's too big to go over my knee,' Estelle stated, defiantly.

'Then stop hitting him altogether,' Bruce replied, raising his voice to match hers. 'Monty loves you and he'll do anything to please you. He—'

Estelle stepped forward, pushed her husband against the wall and slapped his face with all her force.

'Shut up and stay shut up,' she shouted, 'unless you want what he gets.'

She walked out of the kitchen with a grimly muttered 'I've finished with both of you' and went into the double bedroom, slamming the door behind her. Cameron remained, statue-still, his fingers caressing his smarting cheek, not needing to hide his gratification from his stepson because the kneeling boy was still facing away from him. Presently, he crossed the floor, helped Monty to his feet and said gently: 'Come on! Let's talk in your room.'

'There's a letter for you in the office, Ibzy. Blanchard Brothers,' the boy said, drying his eyes. The snivelling was dying away. 'It came with mine while you were out.'

In his bedroom, he lay down slowly on his stomach, his palms flat on his pillow, his chin resting in the space between. He shook his head when Bruce asked if he would like some cold cream to massage into his backside.

'Mama had only just started.'

'Since when has she been using a cane on you?'

'I've never seen it before.'

'Is there anything you want? A hot drink? Coffee perhaps with a shot of whisky in it.'

'I'm all right. I hope you've got the London job, Ibzy.'

When Bruce told his wife that he had, she made no reply. She was standing facing the sitting room fire, staring at the flames without seeing them, her arms tightly folded beneath her neat bust, one thigh slightly forward inside her skirt. Coming up behind her and

166

pressing her to him, Cameron kissed her ear, confiding his love for her. She didn't apologise then or later for slapping his face and he didn't want her to, since an apology would have diluted the pleasure she had given him. With closed eyes, he swayed her gently in his arms, kissing her cheek and neck, murmuring endearments, savouring the possibility that she could in future be provoked into treating him as she had treated Clyde Beaumont.

'Monty didn't fail on purpose, Estelle,' he whispered.

No answer.

'He loves you, Estelle, as I love you, and he would never have done that to you. He's your son, okay, but in some ways I know him better than you do. There's no guile in Monty – in your friend, perhaps, but not in your son.'

'I'm going back to Canada,' Estelle said, irritably, still gazing into the fire. 'Monty can come with me or stay here with you. He's old enough now to make up his own mind.'

Bruce turned his wife round to face him.

'Monty will go with you,' he said, smiling at her. 'The only question is – can I come too?'

Estelle hesitated, frowning on the edge of disbelief. She asked if he was serious.

'Never more so.'

'But what about this London appointment?' she asked, moodily. 'You've worked for it and now it's yours. Are you saying you don't want it after all?'

'I'm saying I want you. Can't you find room for me in the family firm? Salesman? Manager? Me with my sales experience, my command of French, thanks to you, and my marketing diploma.'

'You'll be working for me.'

'Righty, as you would say.'

'Not every man likes working for his wife.'

'Not every man has a wife like mine.'

Estelle, amused by this unexpected and not unwelcome turn of events, teased soft brown hair away from one eye, tilted her head a little and smiled at her husband as at a new and novel discovery. His lips found hers, she yielded, and never had his kiss been slower, never his spirit more at peace.